THE FOURTH LEVEL
DEEP FREEZE
BOOK SEVEN

NICHOLAS HUNTLEY

"Hidden in wonder and snow, or sudden with summer / This land stares at the sun in a huge silence / Endlessly repeating something we cannot hear."

– Francis Reginald Scott

Act 1, Scene 1

A thin deposit of crystalline dew stuck against the windows of shops on the street level of downtown Harlech. The extra layer that coated the glass was unmoved by the stare of the sun in the clear orange autumn sky. Apathetic pedestrians walked in either direction, most yearning to return home. However, past the glass of the display of the Chamberlain Department Store was a breadth of warmth that attracted those with deep hearts. Inside was a joyous demonstration of holiday cheer with cotton snow laid beneath the porcelain model of a small village and the feet of a gregarious Santa Claus with his royal red robe and burly black burlap bag around his right shoulder.

The porcelain figure of Father Christmas looked straight across the street from the store display to Dominion Square in front of the Royal Harlech Museum of Natural History where a tall evergreen tree stood in the center. The three was decorated in burgundy ribbon, regal ornaments, and large decorative boxes of gifts as well as furious protesters with picket signs in all sorts of profanities.

A cold tone existed in the air at all levels of the central heart of the metropolitan region. Trees along the sidewalk were bare. Concrete and asphalt stood exposed from any form of snow. The morale of civilians was low and careless.

Along Campbell Street drove a small convoy of vehicles, unescorted and all in black. Two SUVs led the charge with three sedans behind. The windows of the vehicles were tinted to hide the figures within.

The passenger of one of the vehicles was blinded in darkness from his surroundings, clutching a briefcase with both arms for comfort and the sake of holding onto what was his. The man breathed at a calm pace with the limited space around him. The car continued to drive to its destination with him as its passenger.

The cars eventually arrived at a location that was unknown to this certain passenger. The inertia of the vehicles coming to a halt caught him, causing him to develop a nervous sweat. The door to his side opened, and a pair of hands grabbed him by the right arm to pull him out.

The man stuck a foot out as soon as he was out of the vehicle, stepping onto a hard floor with his Italian leather shoes. Another pair of hands took him by the other arm, and the two men escorted him away from the vehicle. The sound of the car door slamming shut could be heard behind him. The ground at his feet was a soft gravel before turning to a hard concrete. The passenger was stopped soon after and assisted up a set of staircases. He then heard a set of large doors opening.

The temperature around him changed from a natural cold to an artificial warmth. The men at his side continued to escort him along a smooth surface of what could have been a carpet atop of hardwood floor. His steps made an echo, which told him the space beneath him was hollow. There was also a musty smell in the air. A ding could be heard and some doors opened. The man was brought forward and then turned around. The doors shut. The floor at his feet moved upwards. The doors then opened again. The man was brought forward.

The man walked for several meters before turning right, left, and then right. He then heard a set of doors opening again. He was brought forward again and then stopped. The men at his side left and the bag over his head was raised, exposing his pale face.

Charlemagne looked ahead of him where several figures in black robes and faceless masks over their faces stood behind a raised platform before him. A central figure stood behind a podium at the center of the platform in the same garb. Additional steps behind these people held additional figures in black robes, but without any masks on. Instead, they wore hoods over their heads and the darkness of the room masked their faces. These figures also bore an emblem at their lapel of what looked to be either a pointed red heart or of red horns brought together.

The room around him was regal. The carpet was formal and bore an interesting post-modern design of various dark colors. The room was mostly empty from side to side. The walls were composed of a dark oak panel for the bottom half, while the top half was made of stone. On either side was a set of three stained-glass windows, but at the current hour, little light poured through. The room was instead lit by candle light – not from the chandeliers on the ceiling, but candelabras on tables and posts.

Behind Charlemagne was a set of double doors from where he came from with two guards in two-piece black suits. Each of them had hair, but also sunglasses despite being indoors. They also had earpieces attached to their right ears.

Ahead awaited a table for Charlemagne to stand behind. He stepped forward and made his approach, setting his briefcase atop of the table before looking up to the figures in masks.

"Charlemagne de la Cabernet," the central figure said in a deep Italian accent. "We thank you for returning so that we can review and conclude this agreement between the Committee of Concerned Nations and those of which you have chosen to represent, including yourself and your own children: one, Tristan Luke Merrick, and the other, Diana Anne Cambridge. Are you still in agreement to act as representative of those of your staff members that participated in the events that took place this year between August 25th and September 3rd with the exception of Dr. Bartholomew Nathaniel Lambert, who we understand, is no longer under your employment. Is this correct?"

"It is correct," Charlemagne replied in a stern, loud voice.

"Is it also correct that you hold no information as to the current whereabouts of Dr. Bartholomew Nathaniel Lambert?"

"It is correct."

"And is it correct that the former spouse of Dr. Bartholomew Nathaniel Lambert, Dr. Judith Athena Lambert holds no information as to the current whereabouts of her ex-spouse."

"It is."

"Do you continue to pledge responsibility for the actions of all those you have chosen to represent, but are not present here?"

"I do."

"And do you agree to review the provisions of our agreement of which you will be agreeing upon with these individuals in the presence and witness of at least one of our peacekeepers?"

"I do."

"Do you and your party intend to recognize the provisions of the Treaty of Roswell, which includes, but is not limited to a pledge of silence, secrecy, and public denial to the existence of extraterrestrial lifeforms lest you are punished under section 9(1) of the treaty which grants the government of your country of origin the right to punish you for the crime of treason or any other related crime. Is this correct?"

"We do."

"Do you and your party intend to recognize the provisions of the Treaty of Juneau, which brought peace between this world and the other world out there this year?"

"We do."

"Do you and your party intend to deny involvement with and the existence of the Global Defense Project as well as the Guardian Initiative?"

"We do."

"Do you pledge to cease any and all activities having to do with research, information gathering, data collection, as well as communication and contact with all extraterrestrial lifeforms and civilizations."

"We do."

"And finally, in relation to the disappearance of former Director of Operations Fumu Selebi, do you confirm that the testimony given to this committee to be authentic and that it is therefore true that you hold no information or knowledge as to the current whereabouts of this man?"

"I do."

"And you hold no information into his escape from custody of the Global Defense Project or the various documents stolen by this man after his disappearance on September 3rd of this year?"

"I do not."

"Very well," the figure replied. "Let it be known in this room at this moment of the gratitude this council has for you and your assistance in maintaining world peace. There, however, lies one last provision to our agreement that has yet to be discussed and has come to light only recently."

"Mr. Cabernet," a separate figure said to the right in a feminine voice, "as a citizen of Canada (a member-state of this committee), the Canadian government seeks an additional clause to our agreement. With your approval, the current government wishes access to all documents surrounding the divisions of Cabernet Industries, including Cabernet Space, to monitor –"

"No, no, no," Charlemagne muttered over her.

"—in order to monitor their activities out of concern for public safety, which has proven to the current government to be of… most concern, Mr. Cabernet."

"No!" Charlemagne rejected.

"Do you agree to this clause?" the woman asked.

"You have no right!" he shouted at the figures. "You thieves have no right!"

"Mr. Cabernet," the central figure said. "Should you not agree then to our offer of amnesty and agreement, then it will be terminated. You will be prosecuted for treason and obstruction of justice. You *will* go to jail. Do you understand this?"

Charlemagne swallowed his breath. He looked angrily at the figures, took a deep sigh, and looked to the side in silence.

"It is a measure to ensure that you, a man that has shown us to be quite predictable and the owner of a corporation that has been quite rebellious, can uphold the provisions of this treaty as well as those associated with you," the woman stated. "We cannot allow a Canadian citizen and your corporation, a Canadian business, to be included in this secret simply because of your role in saving the world. It is the duty of our government as a member-state of this committee to keep yourself and your company in check for the sake of the international world."

"With all due respect, Cabernet Industries respects the local and international law to the last letter in all its operations and situations," Charlemagne argued and scoffed. "You call my business rebellious, but we are merely rebellious from your clutches of this clique of elites because our incentives have never been the same. You see a profit in this world – a world in which you seek to profit from. That is your desire for peace (peace so long as it benefits you) and status quo because it is a status quo in which you will and only ever will be able to benefit from. For when you no longer can, you are not peaceful people, but murderous warmongers that will force peace upon those that you can profit from. I acted last September on moral grounds; morals that are lost upon you. We do not see eye to eye; eyes of which should not be on me. It should be you who has eyes kept on... It is not a matter of public concern, so do not dare to lie to me with your rhetoric and excuses. It is your own private concern and interest to keep me in 'check' and not a threat to you as opposed to the common citizen."

"Do you accept these provisions or not, Mr. Cabernet?" a third figure asked in a French accent.

"What choice do I have?" Charlemagne bitterly replied. "Of course, but not out of my own freedom. I accept them because you have given me no other choice."

Charlemagne turned to see two figures in black suits arrive at his side with a briefcase in one hand. These figures were distinct from others as they were not agents of the Global Defense Project, or 'men in black.' The agent with the briefcase raised the case up and opened it. Inside was a velvet surrounding alongside a piece of paper and pen.

The agent set the briefcase on the table. Charlemagne looked at the Treaty of Harlech as it was titled. He picked up the pen after glimpsing through the document and then signed. The agent then closed the briefcase and took the pen off of him. He then walked off.

"On this date of December 5th, let the provisions of the Treaty of Harlech come into effect and international law," the central figure said. "Let us ensure that we never meet again, Mr. Cabernet."

Charlemagne looked at the figure distastefully.

"Of course, that will be most unlikely. Dismissed."

The central figure hit a gavel on his podium. Charlemagne turned to leave, but before he could finish turning around, the suits had already come to him and brought a black bag over his head.

Act 1, Scene 2

Diana slapped her hockey stick down and onto the ice, prompting Tristan to drop the puck in his hand onto the rink.

"Come on, let's end this tie already," Diana taunted.

Tristan shook his head from side to side with a grin, dropping the puck with his nerves charged to pounce on it before Diana. Alas, he wasn't fast enough as Diana pre-empted his play and blocked his stick before going for the puck herself. Diana skated away from him and made her way to the other side of the rink, going for Tristan's unprotected net as he chased her from behind. Tristan intercepted, skating as fast as he could to take the puck from his girlfriend before turning around to go for the other unprotected net.

Diana struggled to turn around and go after her, but still hurried, dropping onto her side to slide into Tristan as he lined up to take a shot in Diana's net.

"What the hell?" Tristan remarked as he fell over and onto the ice. "Did you just drop kick me?"

"No," Diana lied, standing up to go swipe the puck as Tristan sat on the ice.

Tristan watched as Diana skated back to the other side, shot the puck into Tristan's net, and then made her way to come back over to Tristan. She shredded some ice towards him as he braked, looking down at Tristan as he simply sat in defeat.

"No way. I want a rematch," Tristan demanded.

"I'm hearing some sore loser talk from you," Diana simply replied with a smile.

Tristan didn't reply and instead took Diana's hand to be helped up. The two of them were skating on a small public ice rink a part of the annual Allabrese Christmas Carnival at Wilshire Park, within St. Allan's Plains on a flat plain of land near the river bank. It was a quiet Tuesday afternoon with little people around and little attractions open.

At the current hour, it was already dark outside, but the park had been artificially lit by the bright lights around, some festive and some practical. Other than the ice rink, there were ice sculptures left behind from the ice sculpting competition last weekend, and a hill not too far from the rink where some children were sledding.

Diana and Tristan skated to the edge of the artificial ice and hopped over the ledge to step into the snow in their skates. Each of them had started to strip the shin pads they were wearing over his rugged hockey sweatpants and her ski pants from Russia that kept them warm.

"You move pretty swiftly for someone that's just learned how to skate this weekend," Tristan remarked.

"Yeah, I'm just that kind of gal, Tristie," Diana replied.

"Yeah, I am a great teacher, aren't I?" Tristan added with a smirk. "I've taught you how to ski, how to ride a horse, swim, what else?"

"I get it. You don't need to be such a show-off," Diana said, cutting him off as she removed her skates. "No less do you need to remind me of the upbringing I had compared to you where I was too busy learning how to fend for myself and my mom than to indulge in a life of leisure."

"Hey, take it easy. I didn't mean it that way," Tristan replied, removing his own skates. "I like teaching you. I do. It's nice. It gives us something extra to do and bond over. Plus, it's intimate."

Diana took a picture of Tristan sat in the snow with Tristan's smartphone as he finished talking, giving a smile of disbelief as he yanked his phone back into his own hands.

"You know, you could always ask Charles to buy you your own phone," Tristan remarked as he looked at the picture before stashing his phone into his jacket. "Christmas is not too far off and he was hinting at us to give him some gift ideas."

"I don't know," Diana complained. "I don't want to turn into an addict like you. I hate addictions. If somebody has something to say to me, I prefer if they talked to me in person rather than hide behind a screen."

"You and Moira talk online all the time. What's the difference?" Tristan pointed out, standing up with his things.

"We don't talk to each other *all* the time, and when we do, it's over video chat. She knows this."

"I still don't understand," Tristan replied, walking over to a path as he waited for a passerby with his phone in hand.

"I mean, I'm perfectly happy without a cellphone," Diana said. "I don't want to become some sort of social media junkie either. I'm happy as I am, spending my free-time reading books instead of obsessing over other people's lives."

"Excuse me, ma'am?" Tristan asked a woman as she passed them.

"Yes?" she replied.

"If it's not too much to ask, could you take a photo of me and my girlfriend?" Tristan politely requested.

"Certainly," the woman replied, taking Tristan's phone in hand as the two walked back a couple of steps to pose.

"You don't want to use social media and yet you use mine," Tristan remarked as they posed with smiles.

"It's not the same," Diana responded. "Besides, somebody has to manage your accounts."

Both Diana and Tristan were dressed for the weather in light winter jackets, boots and knit caps. They both smiled as the photo was taken before walking over to the nice woman.

"Thanks a lot," Tristan said as he took his phone back before putting it away.

"No problem," the woman replied with a smile. "You and your girlfriend make a really cute couple."

Diana blushed as the woman walked off.

"Come on," Diana said to Tristan, taking his hand. "Let's warm up a little before we leave."

Tristan held a warm smile as the two walked down the path.

"I'm surprised you referred to me as your 'girlfriend,'" Diana mentioned. "Usually, it's either friend or sister."

"I mean, you're my adopted-sister technically, even if that phrase does make us uncomfortable. Besides, that's what everybody in this town pretty much thinks of us – which I wasn't thinking at the time when I saw that woman. Hopefully she doesn't identify us as the adopted children of Charles the Great."

"*Blegh*," Diana remarked in disgust. "You as my sibling isn't the image I have in my head when we're hanging out like this."

"It's not incestuous," Tristan protested. "My grandfather married his cousin, but it was okay because they weren't blood-related."

"Would you marry me?" Diana asked out of the blue.

Tristan hesitated to reply as he started to give an awkward smile. He shook his head with a grin before looking away from Diana.

"Too cute," Tristan simply replied.

"That doesn't sound like an answer to me."

"Stupid questions get stupid answers then," Tristan laughed, "but then again, you didn't even think to consider me as your boyfriend until I called you my girlfriend to Moira."

"So, is that a 'yes' then?"

"Hm, it's a maybe."

"Okay, hypothetically then."

"Maybe," Tristan repeated.

"Perhaps you should have just said to that woman that I was your friend, or best-friend instead of girlfriend. There's a likely chance she either knows or will know that we're Charles' kids. I mean, it's not like that's a lie either. Moira aside, you are my best-friend."

"I wasn't going to say to that woman, 'Hey, do you mind taking a picture of me and my best-friend?' was I? Nobody calls their best-friend accordingly so unless they're trying to intentionally stress the fact to someone."

"I see your point," Diana replied as they reached the concessions tent.

"Besides," Tristan replied, whispering to Diana as they paused underneath the heat of the tent, "I think I'm a little scared to challenge Moira to the title. She's pretty defensive of you ever since she's found out about us. I really don't want to have to confront her again, ever."

"She won't tell anyone," Diana assured him. "She only hates you, not me. She wouldn't do that to me."

The couple walked to a table and set their stuff down. Diana took off her hat and fixed her hair. Meanwhile, Tristan took out a thermos from his backpack.

"I don't know why she's upset at me – she entrapped us. She also lied to you, Tristan said. "First, she lied to you about having a crush on me to see if you'd get jealous. Then, she guilted us over hiding something so personal. It's our own goddamn choice about who gets to know that we're dating. I chose nobody, except for a few strangers… but that's beside the point."

"Forget about it, Trist. Think of it as a little extra protection by having somebody we know and trust know about this," Diana said as she took the thermos and unscrewed the lid. "Besides, if anything happens to the either of us, she'll be there to inform someone."

Tristan looked down at the ground before looking to her and saying, "Just no more, please?"

"Relax. You know I'm in agreement with you over this. We're on the same page."

Diana poured Tristan and herself some hot chocolate from the thermos.

"I know," Tristan replied, taking the mug into his own hands as he scratched his forehead. "God, let's talk about something else rather than this crap."

"What about Christmas? What are you hoping for this year?" Diana asked.

"You don't have to get me anything, Diana," Tristan replied.

"I'm not talking about me – I'm talking about Santa Claus."

"Oh right, sorry. I'll be sure to mail my wishlist to dear Saint Nick then," Tristan sarcastically replied.

"Why do you say it like that?" Diana asked.

"What do you mean?"

"You say it like you're not actually going to do it."

"Because I'm not going to do it. I'm not ten. I mean, writing to Santa was something I never even did as a kid. I'm not sure about you though. It sounds like you did it if you say it's some sort of tradition. Am I right?"

"Yeah, of course I did. Why do you think that I love Christmas so much?" Diana questioned him. "Then again, I can understand your distaste for the holiday…"

"Let's not bring that up either, Diana," Tristan requested. "I'm not taken aback by Christmas because of what it's associated with to me."

"We never really did celebrate Christmas last year because of what happened then. There would have also been no possible way for Santa to have found us."

"Stop," Tristan remarked. "You don't actually believe in Santa Claus, do you?"

"What do you mean?" Diana questioned. "Do you not?"

"Uh, no… I'm not ten years old."

"You don't have to be a kid to believe, Trist. I always put my faith in him. I always got nothing for Christmas, but I understood that I wasn't a good kid. To me, it was just a sign that I wasn't a good kid."

"Jeez…" Tristan replied, refraining from laughing as he paused for a moment. "You're just… too cute."

"What?"

"Nothing. I won't spoil it for you." Tristan replied.

"Spoil what?"

The two of them were cut off by the wind that started to pick up outside as it got dark.

"Jesus, is it going to storm again tonight?" Tristan asked as he finished his mug.

"Looks like it," Diana replied. "I almost fell off the bed last night because of how close you were getting to me."

"Sorry, but your room picks up a mean draft – we should get going. I don't want to walk home in the pitch dark when this storm gets worse. Come on."

"Fair enough," Diana replied, finishing her mug before putting the thermos away as Tristan grabbed his things.

The two exited the warmth of the heated tent and found themselves in the middle of the mild blizzard that was creeping upon Allabrese for a second time.

"You know, I love the snow, but in moderation," Tristan remarked aloud as they started to walk to the sidewalk. "It's worse than it was last year.

"Yeah, well, that's the climate for you," Diana replied. "People turn a blind eye to action that could have prevented this from getting worse, but it will get worse."

Tristan rolled his eyes and scoffed.

"Don't be so naïve, Diana," Tristan remarked as they walked along together.

"What do you mean? Please don't tell me you don't believe in climate change."

"I'm not that type of moron. I understand climates can change. I'm just not a brainlet that believes whatever the Fake News tells me to believe in. Everything they want you to believe in about climate change, or 'global warming,' is complete crap, Diana. It's nothing but an end-times fable meant to scare people, especially young people, into guilt to do *whatever* those behind the myth want them to do. Yes, climate change exists but guess what – it's just that. It's something that happens and all the politicians, media businessmen, globalists, and the other landed-elites do is juice it for all the votes, money, and power it can produce. I'm not being biased towards either side of the political spectrum – left and right are the same miserable liberal-democrats that appeal to the ignorant."

"I'm lost. So, you believe in climate change? Then why did you scoff at me like that?" Diana asked as they got further down the road and began to climb a hill to the river bridge. "Surely you'd think that stopping it would be good."

"Diana, you can't stop something as powerful as mother nature. You can't stop or regulate the climate and weather. You can't even predict what the climate is going to change into. We're talking about a force that is far great than all of the West, or even the entire globe. The entire basis of the modern myth is groundless. The association between carbon dioxide and rising temperatures has no correlation, but people believe it because their prophets (scientists) tell them to as if they have some sort of authority. The truth is that nobody knows why the climate changes, and there are plenty of those attempting to investigate the truth. That's what I'm concerned about – the truth. Not a truth or a narrative, but *thee* truth. Look at the entire green lobby – a bunch of upper-class elites and bourgeoise that tell you to eat less meat, drive less, use less hot water, and to use less electricity – the same people who enjoy lavish lifestyles. They're hypocrites that are manipulating honest (and innocent) working class people. Someday, whether we like it or not, the Earth is going to get hot again, and then, it'll get cold again. Why do you think the Ice Age happened? Sure, the effect of climate change is devastating, but it's nothing new nor something that humans are responsible for causing. We are still in the last Ice Age, yes. However, until the last polar ice-caps melt, we will continue to be in an Ice Age. You… you just need to do your own investigation into it, Diana. You need to look into it yourself and see the other side of the debate – look at sources that aren't sponsored by dirty money. I hate to know that you've been lied to."

"I'm not being lied to. Why would I be lied to about something like this? I think you're just being cynical. A lie this big could never take-off for people to believe – something as serious as this could never survive as a lie."

"True, lies never do survive, but that's the thing. You make the assumption that we're at an end. We're not. The lie won't survive because there are people that do question the truth. It won't survive," Tristan said again, sighing. "You really would be surprised at how wrong you really are, my other half."

Act 1, Scene 3

Charlemagne barged into the doors of the Nattau Observatory, hugging himself in his mountain parka as he escaped the blizzard outside and led the way for Judith Lambert behind him. The observatory was dark, cold, and deserted. Charlemagne looked around with saddened eyes at the state of the interior as Judith closed the doors behind them and then found a light switch.

"What is it?" Judith questioned, walking over to him as she put a hand on his shoulder.

Charlemagne's eyes tracked around in nostalgia and memories. A tear formed but was quickly wiped aside as he caught himself.

"Nothing," Charlemagne replied. "I'm just thinking about all the work we have in front of us. You know, you didn't have to come, my dear."

"Nonsense," Judith replied, moving her hands away from Charlemagne. "I couldn't have left all of this on your own, Charles. Besides, I know you're still with fresh guilt and I want to do whatever I can to help you relieve that if we're going to try us again."

"I suppose that it was an unfortunate accident for him, and he did tell me that he needed a push to move on with his life," Charlemagne remarked.

"There you are," Judith said. "You see? There's the optimistic Charles we all love and enjoy."

The lights of the observatory slowly lit up, revealing the mess around. Most of the equipment had already been taken in the move, but some remained against the surrounding walls and created the abandoned atmosphere that the area now carried. On another hand, other areas looked unnatural to an abandoned atmosphere with papers on the floor and drawers torn from the desks.

"I suppose Ms. Black's agents have already been through here," Charlemagne said, "looking for Barry or information into where he could have gone."

The living quarters in the room to the left from the entrance seemed to be mostly ripped of all its furniture. Charlemagne opened the glass shutter door and stepped inside the staff kitchen. He walked past the messy counters and over to Barry's bedroom. He turned the light to see that the bed was still there alongside several possessions, one of which was a picture atop of the dresser.

The bed was unmade, sheets torn back, some clothing still around and of course, there were some files with documents pertaining to Barry's research that were on the floor or in piles. Charlemagne knocked into some empty cans of pop as he made his way to the other side of the room to pick up the picture frame of Barry and Judith on their wedding day. The glass was cracked and the frame was knocked over as though somebody had thrown something blunt at it in a quick rage. Charlemagne picked it up and saw that some pieces of glass had fallen before him. He inserted his hand into the frame and started to dig the pieces out so that he could rip the photo from its confines. He then neatly folded it and placed it in his jacket pocket.

"My God, what a state of affairs this is in," Judith remarked as she turned on the light behind Charlemagne.

"I doubt it was always like this. Barry was never the type," Charlemagne remarked. "I remember he was always quite obsessed in keeping order in our dorm when we lived together. All of this was either those pillagers or him in his rush to run off."

"After all we did to save the world – to mark him as a wanted criminal…" Judith said as she put her arms around Charlemagne's waist.

"He's not a criminal though. He's the last man to be a criminal."

"What do you mean?" Judith questioned.

Charlemagne sighed and tore himself from Judith to walk out.

"He didn't even say goodbye. I had to hear it from the secret organization that Barry had disappeared."

"Yes, well, if you're going to dwell on the past, then you best leave and let me do all the work, Charles. You came her to clean, not sulk. We're going to be here all night, and this is the last place I'd like to spend the night with this blizzard wreaking havoc outside – on my day off no less."

"Of course. I'm sorry, but I did warn you."

"You warned me, but now I'm here to help. I'll search for some garbage bags and you can start in this room while I take the main floor," Judith said.

"Right," Charlemagne replied, dropping the empty picture frame onto the floor so that he could follow Judith out. "My, with this weather, I might have to cancel the Christmas party tomorrow."

"It might be the sensible choice, but I'm sure that it will calm down by tomorrow," Judith said to him. "Don't be too anxious."

"I believe I'm more anxious to let it go down than to cancel it to be quite honest," Charlemagne remarked as he crossed his arms. "With you attending, I don't know what to say in my speech or know what the others are to think of me. I don't know how they'll react to us. I mean, yes, you're divorced, but everybody knows of my friendship with Barry and it'll seem like petty celebrity intrigue to the others – it'll be nothing more than table-top gossip. Perhaps I should just cancel and we can spend the night with the children instead. Something familiar rather than public."

"Charles, this town is our family," Judith replied as she found some black garbage bags. "We can spend a moment with the children some other time, but tomorrow is the night of the town. It is the night that Charlemagne de la Cabernet treats his family to something special at his own expense."

"Right… damn. Why are you always right?" Charlemagne questioned.

"You're too tense, Charles," Judith exclaimed as she handed him a bag. "Perhaps this cleaning will be good for you. When I'm tense at home, I clean. It helps me clear my mind, meditate, and storm ideas while achieving something productive. Now go – clean that bedroom and don't come back until it's spotless."

"Yes, dear," Charlemagne replied.

"And don't worry about the party tomorrow, or about me. I don't care about what others will be saying or thinking about me. I went to high school – I've lived through the worst. I can take whatever this town may say in their worst."

"Yes…" Charlemagne added, taking the bag with him to the bedroom.

Charlemagne got to work, picking up trash and garbage to put into the black bags whilst separating important documents from the mix.

Once Charlemagne was finished, he took the garbage bags to the bathroom and then the kitchen. There wasn't much to do in regard to important information in the mounds of garbage around the living quarters. Judith continued to work in the area, retrieving whatever she could in terms of important documents whilst throwing out all the junk she could find. When Charlemagne was finished, he brought both the trash and the papers with him outside, leaving the garbage outside the door to the living quarters as he went to the pile of folders that Judith had collected.

"What's the most intriguing piece you've found?" Charlemagne asked. "For me, it was some statistics in regard to unidentified flying objects."

"Oh, nothing like that," Judith replied. "I haven't found much in the way of Barry's personal documents. Although, I haven't cleaned out the filing cabinet in the back or even looked inside."

"That's good. I suppose whatever is left inside can remain there. I'll have it transferred to the labs at a later date after the holiday season. Your master key should work on them – they're cabinets from the lab. You can look into what's inside at a later date."

"I'll see to shredding whatever should be shredded later too – not that it matters. Those pesky agents have already infiltrated this sacred space and taken whatever they fancied."

"Yes, it's a minor setback and I wasn't happy about finding out about the break-in either. I don't care if Ms. Black is in charge of that organization, but I don't trust her either. We may have evaded a war, but being at that tribunal... I'm uncomfortable with who those people were, what their goals are, what their desires and interests are.... I understand that Ms. Black has a pure heart – she's shown that by allying with us rather than with Director Selebi. She is a woman of principle, but some of those principles are not the same as my own. It is better for the organization that she is in charge instead of the empty-minded fool before. We'll have to shred anything that could be exposed to them and indict us under those 'treaties' as soon as possible. All other high-value documents will need to be scanned and then uploaded to the servers in the manor for now."

"It's for the best…"

"I'm just… very furious at their implications of sending moles in Cabernet Industries. I'm suspect to believe that the original mole in the company was their own too. I never… I never did tell you about when I first met Ms. Black, did I?"

"No," Judith replied with slight intrigue.

"It was after the uprising on Halloween. She had managed to break into the mansion. She talked to me from outside of my bedroom and demanded that I hand everything I knew about the spirits in addition to the technology I had produced. I refused. She said that she would attempt acquire these items by other means. Between then, my experience in Russia and my experience over the last several months, I have reason to believe that she could be the one behind those events, which could then connect her to Nero Medici and Sergei Bykov. Then again, perhaps not as Sergei and his mercenary friends are connected to Audric Zimmerman, and they had my important documents placed on the black market, which would be an odd move if their intentions were to sell the documents to this secret organization who hardly seem like the type to sell secrets. Therefore, I am more than certain that Audric was the man behind those two."

"Of course…" Judith replied. "No, that makes absolute sense, Charles."

"Aye, we are such a modest corporation, and we have so many enemies. I understand that one cannot eliminate corrupt from the face of the Earth, and I am sure that there are some in my party who are no exempt from that fact, but what this company stands for remains the same and is put into practice as best as we can. We stand for honest leadership and have always been oriented towards the public. I've never cared about profit – not a single Cabernet chairman has ever cared about profits. My father nearly ran this company to the ground with his deficits. I earn my fair salary by the work I put in (even if my role is more a consultant or mascot position). I cannot lower the salaries of the others in management positions – they're experienced professionals in their field and in a competitive market."

"You don't need to tell me, Charles."

"I do, because it's been bothering me. It irks me to see people hate against the company and that secret society come at us from a position of envy and hate. The implications of violating those treaties... it bothers me too. We may be a people-oriented corporation and we may break our fair share of laws when necessary to, but these laws and the watchdogs they're sending... it scares me. All it would take is for some harmless technician working at Kennte to accidentally come across alien life or alien alloys, and those thugs will shut us down, arrest me, take the kids... I can't that handle pressure – I'm not free."

"You don't need to worry about the children, Charles. I'm here for them. I'll always be here for them when you're not," Judith said, taking Charlemagne by the arm.

"Thank you, but they're my weight to uphold."

"I choose to make them my responsibility too."

Charlemagne nodded to her before looking to the side. He looked as though he was about to faint.

"My, that alien alloy... the material we discovered – what a discovery. It was such a light and resistant material. What do you reckon the tensile strength of that material really was? What do you imagine we could build if we have the ability to produce that material on our own?"

"Yes, the alloys the aliens had was quite tough, yet light," Judith replied, letting go of Charlemagne.

"We were ahead of our time, Judy," Charlemagne said. "We built devices that were centuries ahead of what we could ever produce... stealth camouflage, rocket ships that could travel faster than light… we could colonize the Solar System with that they had. However, this volta is exactly what the G.D.P. forbids. Hypocrites… even with the stealth camouflage and alien weaponry they seized. They'll put them into their own use, create their own weapons and their own aircrafts."

Charlemagne and Judith went silent. He then started to wag his finger at Judith.

"You know, if only there were some sort of loophole where we could pursue more of that alien substance… just to research it in the least and then possibly analyze it for our own production. We might… might just be able to perfect the fusion reactor, or…"

"Or?"

"Nothing. I just have a thousand or so ideas into what benefits of having a material like that, or a taste of the technology of these beings had."

"Well, even if we don't have it now, our people will find a way in the future. We are not of lesser intelligence than them, Charles. We're stunted and behind them. We have no idea how old their civilization is compared to ours – they're an advanced people who've practiced eugenics to segregate their former races into separate species, specializing themselves into what they are now."

"Meanwhile, we live in a dysgenic world regressing into norms that insist on addressing a man by female pronouns," Charlemagne scoffed.

"Charles," Judith scolded.

"I would love to learn more about those creatures too," Charlemagne instead said. "*Angelus intelligentes* – they were angels, Judy."

"Yes, they were," Judith replied, "but we don't need them. You are being too anxious, Charles, to jump forward. I am beginning to see slight rationale into what the committee and G.D.P. stand for in keeping the status quo. We should just forget about these aliens and move forward with our lives. We cannot interfere with the natural path we are taking – rest assured, we will get to a point in time, even if it takes a thousand years – we will get to a point where we'll be racing across the stars."

"I hope you're right," Charlemagne replied.

"You need to simply stop being so anxious, Charles. What is with you and anxiety?"

Charlemagne didn't reply. His eyes were to the ground before they wandered to some papers on the table that had slipped past him earlier.

"I won't cooperate with them to the extent that they wish. There'll be a mass exodus of important documents and files from Cabernet Space and Cabernet Technologies into my private servers. If they want access to even the littlest of information, I'll delay the release of information as best as I can. I want every single request to run through me, and I won't approve it until I'm given sufficient detail into the nature of their request. I'll peeve them. There'll be nothing for them to take either."

"Charles, it doesn't sound so wise to antagonize an organization like the G.D.P..." Judith warned.

"It's what I must do. Let us not be deceived, dear: we are today in the midst of a cold war."

Charlemagne felt a vibration from his jacket. He took out his phone and looked at the text message from Mavis. Judith sighed as she looked at Charlemagne.

"Right, well, all I can do for you as your girlfriend is offer my full support, Charles. I know one thing for sure, and that's that these miscreants won't be wreaking havoc in my labs."

"Thank you, my dear," Charlemagne replied, smiling at her. "I just received a message from Mrs. Quinn about supper. She also says that the children have returned home from school, which has reminded me… would you be able to take Diana out for another driving lesson tomorrow? I believe she's enjoyed her time with you and I'm no good in making conversation with her. It would help me a lot. I could use the time tomorrow to prepare for the party."

"Yes, of course I'll spend time with Diana," Judith replied.

"Thank you," Charlemagne responded, smiling to her as he put his phone away and walked to her. "You are good with her. I think she likes you more than she likes me. I'm happy with it."

"Diana is a bright young lass with a deep-heart, Charles. You just need to be in the right tune with her," Judith replied, letting Charlemagne hold her as they looked at each other before giving a light kiss.

Act 1, Scene 4

Diana and Tristan stood behind the railing on the second-floor of the manor foyer, looking down towards the guests as Charlemagne concluded his annual Christmas speech. Approximately half of the town was in the mansion at once with the majority in the foyer at the moment. The kids kept an eye on Charlemagne, dressed in a pristine black tuxedo and Judith in a luxurious red dress with her light blonde hair let loose. Her cheeks were red with rouge and she was looking more beautiful than ever as she stood at the side of her boyfriend. The two of them were walking down the stairs on the opposite side of the foyer (the side that went into the library).

Diana wore a sky blue high neck dress that went to her knees. She also had her hair styled (with the help of Judith) to the side. Tristan was convinced by Charlemagne to wear a proper black suit this time, but Tristan wore his without a tie and instead the top button open. Tristan's hair was cut short since September. It was about half an inch in length on the sides and two inches in length at the top.

"You know, I never took Charles as the romantic type," Diana remarked.

"I didn't take you to be the romantic type either," Tristan said in his defense.

"Who said I was romantic?" Diana questioned.

"Fair point," Tristan replied with his eyes following where Judith and Charlemagne were going.

The couple had made their way down the stairs and were ambushed by the power couple, Mr. and Mrs. Huxley, or as Tristan knew them, the parents of his ex-friend and ex-girlfriend. Tristan's eyes wandered away from the four and focused on Peter who looked different than he did last April – he was back from his first semester at the University of Harlech. Vivian was with him. She was dressed in a dark white dress while Peter was in dark trousers, a white shirt and a black tie.

"You know, if they keep this up, we might have a full pair between Charles and her," Diana observed aloud.

"A complete family," Tristan agreed. "I know."

"With Mavis as the sweet grandmother…"

"It doesn't matter to me that much," Tristan remarked as he moved his eyes away from the Huxley family. "I have you. I never asked for more because I'm happy with what I have."

"Thanks," Diana replied with a soft and warm smile, "but we may say that we don't need it, but we do. It's healthy."

Downstairs, Charlemagne continued to chat with both Richard and Jacqueline Huxley. His eyes then turned behind the couple as he noticed a pair of lights flash into the room from the driveway. Diana saw the flash of the light and walked around to peak out a window. She saw a taxi cab pull up the door with a woman stepping out, noticeable by the high-heels. She wore a coat over an elegant turquoise dress she was wearing. Diana then walked back over to Tristan as she heard a knock on the door.

Mavis opened the door and the mysterious figure was welcomed inside. She handed her coat to Ms. Quinn and then looked around.

"Allodia!" Charlemagne said, cutting Richard off as he spoke to him. "Sorry, Ralph, but my sister just arrived. I had no idea she was coming around."

"Allodia?! My God, I haven't seen her in months!" Richard remarked.

Richard and Jacqueline turned around to face Allodia as she looked around the busy foyer before seeing Charlemagne wave over to her. She made her way over to them.

"Allodia, what are you doing here?" Charlemagne asked as he walked over to embrace his sister. "Merry Christmas!"

"Merry Christmas to you too, Charlie. I wanted to surprise you, and I had just enough time in my schedule to pop over to see you and the kids."

"Come," Charlemagne said, leading her over to the others.

"Hello, Allodia," Richard remarked, shaking her hand.

"Hello, Richard," she replied before turning to Jacqueline. "Jacquie, how are you?"

The two greeted each other with cheek kisses, pressing each side of their cheek against the other and making kissing noises. They then parted and Allodia turned to Judith.

"And of course, you remember Judith, don't you?" Charlemagne asked, presenting his girlfriend to his sister.

"Of course," Allodia replied, going to her to greet her with cheek kisses as well as shaking her hand. "How are you, doctor?"

"Exceptionally well, Allodia," Judith greeted in her usual elegant accent.

"That's the spirit," Richard remarked. "Your dear brother has been treating her well, and at the pace those two are going, you might be looking at your new sister-in-law."

"Ralph…" Charlemagne scolded.

"Well, isn't it true, Charles?" Judith questioned, looking to him.

"Sister-in-law?" Allodia questioned, turning her head at Judith. "Are you dating Salmar? I can't think of any brother of mine that would date ever again."

"Yes, she's in a long-distance relationship with Sal is the case," Charlemagne replied with equal sarcasm.

"Well, I'm happy for the two of you – you and Charlie, I mean," Allodia remarked. "I'm also surprised either of you had found the time for romance, but then again, I'm standing next to Richard and Jacquie who have shown us how to make it work."

"Yes, eighteen years and two more to our twentieth anniversary," Richard laughed. "Tell me, though, Allodia. How has the Cabernet Foundation been? I rarely have the time to keep up with them."

"All is well thanks to the steady income from the father-organization."

"What are the next plans for the team then?" Richard asked.

"Oh, we have an arctic expedition set for departure in close to two days."

"Ah, is it for wildlife recovery?" Jacquie questioned.

"I wouldn't think so," Judith answered. "At this time of the year, what could they find?"

"That's right," Allodia affirmed, nodding. "We're just doing a simple mission up north to deliver some supplies to the local communities. It is a minor operation before the end of the year and then I'll be back in Harlech for the rest of January."

"The arctic…" Charlemagne said, pausing for a moment. "I suppose you'll have a small crew for an operation that size."

"Yes, only my most trusted companions with the charity. We don't have much space nor the need for so much manpower. Your friend Dr. Vidkunsen is joining us, however, as our physician."

"Good," Charlemagne said, nodding.

"Cabernet Foundation has always been a small group of individuals. It's the smallest division in the whole company – only twenty of them in total," Richard explained.

"Right," Charlemagne said. "You wouldn't mind taking an additional crew with you if you could?"

"Are you volunteering to join us, Charlie? You're always welcomed to join me on an expedition," Allodia remarked.

The adults laughed while Charlemagne simply smiled and nodded.

"The arctic is an interesting place…" Charlemagne commented, "… lots of mysteries to be found, especially under all those glaciers."

"The best time to have an adventure in the arctic would be in the summer," Allodia suggested. "There's nothing to see in the winter and we're not going for sightseeing. It's just a simple mission to several of the island ports along Nunavut and Greenland."

"Yes, I'll keep that in mind, but for now, if you'll please excuse me," Charlemagne said, bowing his head and stepping back.

"Where are you going?" Judith questioned.

"I'll be right back," he said. "I just need to pop into my study for a brief moment. I'll be back for the other guests soon. Keep them entertained for me until then."

Charlemagne winked at Judith before turning around to go into the library, leaving Allodia with Judith and the Huxley couple.

"I'm sorry about him," Judith said, turning to the guests.

"No need, doctor," Richard replied. "I'm used to it. After all, it's Charles we're dealing with. Anyways, Allodia, it was a pleasure to see you again. I wish the best for you and the foundation team. Merry Christmas."

"Merry Christmas, Allodia," Jacqueline added.

Both Mr. and Mrs. Huxley left Allodia with Judith. Allodia turned to her and smiled.

"So, you and Charlie, eh?" she said with a bit of surprise.

Tristan observed.

"Where does Charles think he's going?" Tristan questioned Diana.

"I don't know, but I'm starting to get hungry. Let's go to the ballroom and eat."

"Sure, in a moment," Tristan replied as Diana took his hand. "Let's do some sleuthing first though. Come on."

Tristan led Diana downstairs where they pushed through the crowd and made their way to Allodia. He attempted to bypass her, but instead led himself into the gaze of Judith.

"Ah, children," Judith said, causing them to freeze. "Aren't you going to say 'Hello' to Allodia before you wander off like your guardian?"

Allodia turned to look at the kids. Her face lit up in a beautiful smile as she saw the kids for the first time in almost a year.

"Oh my God," she said, going to each of them to hug them. "You've both grown so much! How are you?"

"Good," Tristan replied as she hugged him.

"Good," Allodia responded, letting go to hug Diana.

"Yeah, we're good," Diana also said.

"How has school been?" Allodia asked.

"Oh, you know, the same," Tristan answered.

"Good," Allodia responded. "I don't suppose you have long until winter break then."

"Next week is our last," Tristan said.

"Excuse me, Dr. Lambert?" an older gentleman said, cutting into the conversation to talk to Judith. "Have you seen Charlemagne? My wife and I can't seem to find him."

"Oh, yes, doctor," Judith replied, taking a step back. "Charles has stepped out for a moment. Let me go fetch him for you. Please, wait here."

Judith walked off, leaving the children alone with their aunt for a brief moment until Tristan started to edge himself away.

"Actually, I need to see Charles about something too," Tristan remarked. "Sorry…"

"Oh, by no means, Tristan," Allodia said. "You have no obligation to be around me…"

"Thanks," Tristan replied, pulling Diana with him as they escaped into the corridor before the library.

The two of them entered the library and saw Judith escape into the study, closing the door behind her without spotting the others. Both of them went over to the door, but didn't open it to instead eavesdrop from the other side as Tristan got down on one knee to put his ear against the door.

"What are you doing, Charles?" Judith asked, walking over to a table in the middle of the study.

Various documents, blueprints and other items were scattered across the table in the middle. Some of the documents were the ones recovered from the observatory yesterday, and they included reports written by Barry and his team. Charlemagne had two fists apart and against the table, head bent over with his reading glasses on, reading carefully before turning over to the gaze of his woman.

"Judy," Charlemagne greeted, standing up properly as she came over to his workstation.

"What's all this, Charles?" she questioned.

"Nothing important," he replied, "but I had a 'eureka' moment while I was talking to my sister. It's been bothering me… letting ourselves in the dark to the advances that wait before us. Barry and I always spoke about taking the opportunity to launch ourselves forward, and even with this treaty, I don't see why we should be left behind when we're needed."

"What are you talking about, Charles?"

"I want to go to the arctic with my sister… to fool the Global Defense Project and search for more of these alloys. I looked at some of the data Barry had collected, and just before the incident late last summer, he was tracing meteors that had crashed onto the Earth, isolating the regular meteorites from the ones similar to the one that crashed in Allabrese. He had gone through ten years of data and two-hundred rocks that fall on this Earth each year and deduced that about twenty of them could be irregular meteorites – ones composed of alien alloys – with the most recent landing last spring. It appears that the aliens have been leaving us with their garbage."

Charlemagne took a sheet of paper before him on the desk, picked it up, and turned it around to show Judith.

"With this recent meteorite included, there could be two to three sources of alien alloys in the arctic, and that's if this was just the beginning," Charlemagne said, removing his glasses. "In Egypt, the fireball we traced was in reality an alien vessel made of the same material. The arctic is renowned for being a place to find meteorites because of its uniform geography and isolation. I'm going to dig for more information after the party, but with these moles within the ranks of my company, I won't be able to form a traditional expedition. I'll need to disappear with the foundation, fool the G.D.P., and go on my own in secret."

"Now? So soon? Charles, it's nearly winter solstice and also Christmas," Judith replied, lowering the sheet of paper onto the table. "Can't you do this in the summer?"

"No, I need to do this now," Charlemagne begged. "The alloy we discovered has a density lighter than water and combined with the fact that most of the arctic ocean freezes over in the winter, now is the best time to go looking for these rocks because they're immobilized. I'll need some seafloor charts and other documents, which I believe I can request from the University of Harlech, but now is the time to strike. The G.D.P. could… they could be conducting their own similar operation. If that's true, they'll either be on the hunt or have hunted this latest deposit."

"Charles, calm down a little. You're as anxious as a school boy, dearie."

"Sorry," Charlemagne replied, giving an embarrassed smile as he looked down at his girlfriend. "I'll tell you what, love. I'll go, but I'll conduct a preliminary investigation. I won't be gone for long and I'll be back for Christmas. I promise you – you'll see me at the latest before the year end – maybe in the first week of January."

Judith frowned. She then sighed and crossed her arms.

"Fine, Charles. I see the importance in this, and I suppose it won't hurt to investigate," Judith decided, uncrossing her arms.

Judith put her arms around Charlemagne and brought him closer.

"Now then, if you're done scheming, you have guests that would like your attention. Don't be rude – let's not keep them waiting."

"Aye, I suppose so," Charlemagne replied, nodding.

Judith gave Charlemagne a quick kiss before the two parted, taking each other's hands and walking to the door.

"Crap, I think they're coming," Tristan remarked as he heard gaining footsteps. "Quick, hide."

Tristan pushed Diana forward, taking her down the aisle and towards a couch for them to hide behind. Each of them leapt over, crouching down and ducking as they heard the door of the study open. They remained hidden as they heard footsteps pass by from one side of the room to the other. A door opened and the couple could hear ambience from the party. The door then closed. Tristan counted to five and then poked his head up to see if they were gone. Sure enough, they were.

"So, I guess we won't be seeing Charles for the next few days then," Diana remarked, raising her own head up. "That's fine with me."

"He's just going to ditch us again? Like he did when he went to Spain?" Tristan replied, raising himself up.

"I can't believe I'm the one that has to say this, but we have school, Tristan," Diana said to him. "I'm sure Charles would take us if he could."

"Please, what are we doing in class right now? Nothing. It's going to be just like last year when we spent an entire week doing nothing in anticipation for the break. Maybe we'll miss something important in one or two classes, but that'll be it."

"Charles isn't going to take us regardless," Diana replied, standing up.

"Well, maybe we don't need his permission… at least to start with. Come on, why are you against ditching school all of the sudden? Let's check out the arctic, even if it doesn't sound that exciting, it's an experience in the least. Right?"

"I'm not concerned with school. Like you said, it's going to be a breeze until the break. I'm thinking about the alone time we might have with Charles out of the mansion."

"Charles never posed a threat to us having time to spend together to begin with, Diana. It's Mavis I'd be more worried about, or Judith now. Think about it – it didn't sound like 'Judie' was too eager to join Charles, so that might mean she'll stay back here. If she's stuck here, that'll mean she's watching over her two future adopted-children. I doubt we'll have any alone time then."

"Right…"

"And besides, I have another incentive for you. You were just telling yesterday about how you think climate change could be stopped and how you believe in the global warming myth. You need to see a little realization with your own eyes."

"What do you mean?" Diana replied, squinting at Tristan.

"I'm just saying that maybe you'll realize that going toe-to-toe with mother nature is a futile endeavor. You shouldn't have anything to worry about if you're so confident in your beliefs, right?"

"No, you're right. I don't have anything to fear. After all, if we're going to the arctic then perhaps we can take the opportunity to go to the north pole and prove to you that Santa is real," Diana stated. "How about that?"

"You want to hedge your bet on the idea that Santa Claus might be real?" Tristan questioned with a smile, crossing his arms. "Santa Claus, the mascot of selling cocaine-laced soda?"

"You have nothing to fear if you're so confident in your beliefs," Diana remarked, mocking Tristan.

"You're right. I don't. You've got yourself a deal."

"Good," Diana replied, smiling as she crossed her own arms. "Good."

Act 2, Scene 1

Two days later on the following Monday, ripe in the morning, Charlemagne drove his faithful black sedan out to Allabrese airfield where Hank Bond awaited him with his jet. Judith rode in the passenger seat, and Diana and Tristan rode in the back after they insisted on seeing Charlemagne off. Each of them had their backpack so that Judith could drive them to school afterwards. Between the couple was a large duffel bag containing Charlemagne's items for him to take onto the plane to Harlech.

A light amount of snow trickled down, creating acceptable conditions for a takeoff. The runway had been cleared and salted, and the jet sat ready with the airstairs extended. Charlemagne drove right up to the jet, pulled up the parking brake and shifted gears to stall the car. He left the engine running and opened the door as Hank made his way over to greet Charlemagne.

The kids opened their doors and Tristan took Charlemagne's luggage with him as he tried to get out of the car.

"Not so fast," Judith remarked to them.

Each of them stopped as they sat at the edge of their seats, ready to get out of the car.

"Don't think I didn't notice the extra bags in the trunk before we left," Judith said.

"What do you mean?" Tristan replied.

"I know you intend to go with him, and I know that he doesn't intend the same," Judith explained, opening a face powder mirror to do some makeup as she looked at herself in the mirror. "Charles has left me in charge of you two until he returns, and that includes driving you to school and an assortment of other parental responsibilities."

"We really want to go," Diana explained. "It's important, and besides… we're barely doing anything in school at the moment."

"Yeah, this might be more educational than one last week at school might be. You've got to let us!"

"I never intended on stopping you," Judith replied, closing her mirror and blusher. "Why don't you two get the luggage in the back and I'll go talk to Charles to distract him."

"Wait, you'll help us?" Tristan questioned. "And you won't say anything to him? Why?"

"I have my reasons," Judith simply replied, opening her door to go over to Charlemagne. "Now get moving."

Tristan looked over to Diana, and the two got out of the car and hurried to the back to get their bags. Each of them had their backpacks around their shoulders and were now picking up their luggage as Judith walked over to Hank and Charlemagne at the base of the stairs. She embraced Charlemagne for a moment before letting go as she brought her hands to his cheeks.

Diana took his bag out, and the two closed the trunk as the adults talked over the sound of the jet engines. The two of them carried their things towards the stairs, passing behind the adults as they conversed so they could hop up and place their things in the closet immediately next to the entrance. Tristan closed the door and then made his way down behind Diana, reaching the bottom where they faced Charlemagne.

"Hey, Charles," Tristan said. "Where do you want your things to go?"

"Oh, anywhere, Tristan. Just don't hide them, please," Charlemagne replied. "It's only a twenty-minute flight."

"Right…" Tristan replied, walking back to the car with Diana.

"How are we going to sneak in if we're going to have to say goodbye to him?" Diana asked as they got back to the car.

"I don't know," Tristan replied, looking over to the adults as all three of them walked up the stairs. "Just roll with me."

Tristan grabbed hold of Charlemagne's luggage and walked over to the stairs again so that he could walk up and join the adults as they stood near the door.

"Wow, I don't think I've ever been on this plane before," Judith said as the kids arrived.

Tristan brought Charlemagne's luggage around the adults to sit on the opposite from the door. All of the adults stood in the galley of the aircraft, which made Tristan nervous as he looked at the door. Diana thought the same as they looked around, so she made her way into the cockpit.

"I bet you've never seen the cockpit of a jet before either," Diana remarked, prompting all of them to enter.

"No, I haven't," Judith replied.

"Doesn't look as complicated as a space shuttle," Tristan said, closing the door behind him.

"Space shuttle?" Hank questioned.

Charlemagne, Judith and Diana looked at Tristan with judgmental eyes.

"Yes, the Cabernet Space shuttle. I took him onboard for a tour last summer," Charlemagne explained. "Isn't that right?"

"Yeah… a tour," Tristan replied with a sly smile.

"Right, well, unfortunately, if Mr. Cabernet wants to get to Harlech before eight o'clock, we're going to have to leave now," Hank expressed.

"Yes, the kids need to go to school too. Say goodbye," Judith said to them.

"Bye," Tristan said.

"Bye…" Diana also said in a lower tone.

"Bye bye," Charlemagne replied. "Make sure they behave themselves, Judie. I'm sure they will."

"Oh, definitely," Tristan responded, smiling as he nodded his head.

"Alright then, see you, children," Charlemagne said, leading them out of the cockpit.

"Oh, one more thing, Charles," Judith said, stopping Charlemagne from leaving as the kids opened the door and stepped out. "Children, go wait by the car, will you?"

"Can I step out too?" Hank questioned with slight discomfort.

Tristan waited for a moment to make sure Charlemagne wasn't going to get out of the cockpit or Hank for that matter before they took their backpacks from the closet and rushed past the living space and towards the bedroom in the rear of the jet. Tristan locked the door behind them, and then they both made their way over to the bed to sit down, leaving their stuff down on the ground as they both waited with anticipation and anxiety.

"Please, don't let them intimidate you," Charlemagne said to Judith as they broke off from their kiss.

"Oh, don't worry about it, Charles. Everything will be fine," she smiled, opening the door for her herself. "Take care and let me know when you reach Point Alpha."

"I will, my love," Charlemagne replied, meeting her at the door of the plane.

The snow started to pick up a little, but not too much. He could still see around him as Judith carefully made her way to the bottom and over to the car. Charlemagne tried to wave to the kids in the car, but he couldn't see them due to the angle and proximity of the car to the plane. He instead stepped back as the airstairs started to lift up and close so he could go to the cockpit and see for himself as Judith drove off and cleared the runway.

Charlemagne sat down next to Hank as he put on his headset and took a sip of coffee. The plane was facing south. Charlemagne sighed and waited to see the car drive off.

"My, that Judith is quite the woman, isn't she," Hank remarked as he finished his pre-flight check.

"Yes, like you wouldn't believe," Charlemagne said.

Charlemagne saw the car drive off, giving Hank the clearance to turn the plane around and start the takeoff run.

"Are we moving?" Tristan questioned as he continued to sit on the edge of the bed.

Tristan paid close attention to his surroundings. Diana was simply lying on the bed, waiting without a care in the world as she looked over to Tristan. Tristan stood up and walked over to a window. The plane was turning in its place. He looked around for Charlemagne's car, but then the plane started to move forward and gain speed. Tristan took a step back and sat down on the bed as he continued to wait with anxiety.

The jet started its run, gradually increasing and increasing its speed. The cabin started to shake and Tristan knew they were taking off. Diana took a deep breath and closed her eyes as the plane lifted off from the ground. All was safe.

Tristan deliberately fell backwards onto the bed and looked up to the ceiling.

"Wake me up when we get there," he said before turning his back on Diana.

"Sure thing," Diana replied, smiling at him as she moved over to curl up next to him.

Act 2, Scene 2

Diana maintained herself vigilant as the trip from Allabrese to Harlech completed itself in less than fifteen minutes. Without warning, the plane started to descend over the Harlech River and towards Harlech International Airport. Diana looked out of the window as she saw them pass through the clouds at an increasing velocity. She tightened her grip around Tristan, but it wasn't enough to stop them being pushed off of the bed with a brute force of inertia as they touched down.

Charlemagne continued to sit at the front of the plane, writing notes into his personal journal with a beaten pencil as the jet touched the earth. Hank steered the plane into the appropriate zone as he slowed the craft down. Charlemagne put his book away into his blazer and then crossed his arms as he observed the exterior with his own eyes.

"I was hoping I wouldn't have to return to this damned city until the new year," Charlemagne remarked, "and yet, here I am less than four days since my last visit."

"It feels like it was just yesterday," Hank replied as Charlemagne looked ahead to the skyline.

Harlech was still as gray as it was and without a single droplet of snow. The gray clouds stuck around, adding a depressing atmosphere to the city. Hank drove the plane to the private hangar owned by the Cabernet family before letting the engine run as the craft came to a final halt.

"Ah, thank you, my friend," Charlemagne said, standing up as Hank opened the airstairs and then shut down the plane.

"No problem, Mr. Cabernet. Hope you find what you're looking for in the Great White North," Hank remarked, standing up as he removed his headset before following Charlemagne out of the cockpit.

"Oh, and that reminds me," Charlemagne said, turning to him as he grabbed his luggage. "Should any officials from Cabernet Industries phone you asking for me…"

"I won't say a word, Mr. Cabernet," Hank said, giving him a quick salute. "Enjoy your trip and Merry Christmas, sir."

Charlemagne froze for a moment as he looked at him before smiling. He saluted him in return.

"Hopefully I'll see you before Christmas, Hank. Take care and Merry Christmas," Charlemagne said, turning away from him to go down the stairs.

Charlemagne made it to the bottom where a private sedan waited for him with a chauffeur. The driver waited for him outside of the vehicle and opened the door for him. He also took Charlemagne's luggage to bring to the trunk of the vehicle. Charlemagne entered the car and then closed the door. The chauffer returned to the driver's seat and sat down.

Diana watched from the window of the bedroom cabin and saw the car drive off. It left the hangar, cueing the couple to make their leave. Tristan opened the door for Diana, and the two made their way through the middle rooms of the plane to get to the airstairs. The two collected their luggage from the closet.

A cold breeze made its way in from outside as they faced out of the plane. Each of them took steps down the airstairs to the concrete floor of the lonely hangar. They then looked out of the hangar towards the runways of the airport and then around the hangar.

"Right, so how do we do this?" Diana asked Tristan as they reached the ground level.

"Well, we've got to get to Port 3A before the ship leaves," Tristan said as they looked around.

"Yeah, but how exactly do we get out of here without a car or taxi?" Diana questioned, looking ahead of him.

Tristan looked at Diana and saw her concern. He continued to search around before seeing an orange exit sign at a hallway adjacent to the hangar.

"Come on," Tristan said, taking Diana by her hand to lead them down the maintenance corridor.

The two of them came to a door and entered what appeared to be a locker room. The room was lifeless, so they went across to the opposite side where they entered a type of shipping and receiving area with garage doors, forklifts, shelves, and other sorts of equipment. Tristan continued to follow the exit signs, going to the end of the narrow rear of the hangar to enter a door that led them outside.

"I feel stupid carrying all this stuff around like this," Diana remarked as they continued their presence in the airport.

The couple had managed to find themselves outside, but it wasn't enough. They were still within the limits of the airport, and worse, the Cabernet hangar was set up against the coastline. The fence behind the hangar was not only barbed but led them directly into the cold drink of the Harlech River. Tristan tried to see where the main building of the airport was, and when he saw it behind the adjacent hangar, he started to walk again.

"Come on, we'll just have to get out the normal way," Tristan said, walking around the hangar to get a clearer view.

The sight of planes landing nearby on the tarmac they were walking on was unsettling, but they had no other options. They walked the long walk, and as they got closer to the terminals, Tristan saw a security checkpoint that led cars out and into the tarmac zone. He paused for a moment as he looked at the base of the terminal area, seeing no clear door to enter to leave an area they really shouldn't be in. Tristan changed paths and started to walk to the tall chain-link fence where he spotted a gate with a large exit sign.

"Okay, maybe we're going to get out after all," Tristan said, walking a bit faster as he bee-lined for the exit gate.

The two of them pushed through the door in the fence and found themselves in the city. Tristan and Diana walked down the sidewalk next to the checkpoint, down the road, and towards a street known as Park Drive.

"Well, this is your city, Diana. Do you know where we are?" Tristan asked as he looked to either direction cluelessly.

"No... I didn't live on this side of town. I have no idea where we are," Diana confessed.

"Well, I guess we'll have to go back to the airport then..." Tristan remarked.

"I feel like at the pace we're going, we're going to be late," Diana responded as they started to make their way down Park Drive and back towards the airport. "Give me your phone."

Tristan took his cellphone out of his pocket and handed it towards Diana as they started to walk down the road. Tristan kept his eye out for a taxi while Diana brought the phone to her ear.

"Whoa, who are you calling?" Tristan complained, bringing his hand to his phone to take it off her.

Diana dodged out of the way and swatted Tristan's hand away.

"Hello, yes. I need a taxi cab for two please," Diana said into the phone. "We're near the airport, but on a street called Park Drive. Uh... the adjacent street is called... Virtue Street."

Diana hung up in the next few seconds and passed the phone back to Tristan.

"Less than five minutes," Diana said. "Less time than it would've taken us to walk up this hill and all the way to the airport where we'd probably then wait behind other people just for our own taxi."

"Thanks…" Tristan quietly replied, putting his phone away. "You're really showing your street smarts now."

Diana gave a light glare at Tristan for his remark. Tristan gave her a quick kiss on the lips before they locked arms and waited where they were. Park Drive was a quiet street with little passing traffic. The two of them sat atop of their luggage as they waited, and in less than five minutes, the taxi they were promised arrived. It was a yellow mini-van that pulled over at the side of the road where they were to get them back on their journey.

"Where to?" the chauffer, an East Indian man, asked in his deep foreign accent.

"We need to get to Port 3A in Leicester," Diana explained. "Do you know where that is?"

"No," the driver replied, "but I'll go to the harbor in Leicester and look around."

The taxi pulled into the road and started to make its way down to the end of Park Drive before turning, passing underneath a major road and entering into what Diana knew to be Leicester.

"Yeah, this is definitely Leicester alright," Diana remarked, looking out her window as she sat with Tristan in the rear of the car.

It had started to rain as they drove along and entered an unpleasant part of the town with lots of warehouses, dry docks, and Edwardian-era structures that showed their age in one of the oldest parts of Harlech. It had a maritime sentiment and was definitely an improvement over Diana's home district. In other words, Leicester was not a slum, but industrial and rugged. The car passed through, driving underneath another major road to find more warehouses, hangars, mechanical shops, and dry docks. The cab took a left and started to drive down to the waterfront where various brick buildings were lined against the water. Several ships could be seen parked on the harbor, and as they got close, numbers could be seen labelled on the sides of the buildings. The closest numbers were 6B and 7A between two buildings at a T-intersect ahead.

"Go left," Tristan directed. "I think that'll take us to 3A."

The taxi driver turned left, and sure enough, they were taken down the road to find themselves in front of 3A. Each of the ports had their own building, A and B respectively, with causeways going down to the water on the lateral sides. Tristan prepared to pay so he and Diana could get out, get their luggage, and then travel down the causeway as soon as possible.

Unexpectedly, the cab driver turned right and went down the causeway, bringing them right up to the security checkpoint. Tristan immediately unlatched his seatbelt and leaned forward to pay the driver as Diana looked to him and took the hint. She got out of the car and went around to get their things from the trunk. She pulled her hood up and noticed that the rain had gotten hard since their arrival.

Tristan paid the driver and then got out of the car on his own side. He looked over to the checkpoint where a security guard in a yellow reflective jacket stood, looking over to the kids with his hand over his eyes as he squinted at them. Diana handed Tristan his luggage and then the two went forward to confront the guard as he climbed over the road barrier to go to them. The cab pulled back to leave.

"I'm sorry, kids," the guard said to the couple, shouting to compete with noise from the storm, "but this is a restricted area. I'm afraid you're lost and need to turn back around."

"No, we're here to board the vessel!" Tristan replied. "My name is Tristan Merrick and this is my sister, Diana Cambridge. We're the adopted-children of Charlemagne de la Cabernet!"

The guard looked at the two of them with doubt. Diana looked past the guard to where a familiar woman sat at the railing of the icebreaker. She looked at them and took notice.

"Unless you have some sort of documentation that states you're permitted to board this vessel, I'm afraid I'm going to have to ask you to leave," the guard said.

"Don't bother," Diana said to Tristan.

"Huh?" he questioned, looking at her.

Diana looked ahead and saw Allodia walk off and down the ramp to come over.

"What seems to be problem?" Allodia shouted, walking towards them as she went over the road barrier.

"Ms. Cabernet, do you know these children?" the guard questioned.

"Of course. This is my niece, Diana, and this is my nephew, Tristan. You aren't giving them any sort of trouble, are you? Then again, perhaps it's the other way around with these two…"

"No, ma'am," the guard replied to her before looking at the kids. "No trouble here."

"Right," Allodia replied, nodding. "Come on," she added, motioning the kids to follow her.

Diana looked at the guard begrudgingly as he let them walk with Allodia and pass the gate. The three of them were on the docks of Port 3A where it ran a short distance behind the main structure before hitting the water and going inland to the space between the structures of 3A and 3B. A steel ramp with railings branched off from the ground in the middle, going up onto the portside of the ship. Allodia paused and turned around as they got to the base of the ramp onto the boat.

"You guys, what are you doing out here? We're leaving any minute now. Let's get you onboard," Allodia said before turning around again.

Diana and Tristan looked at each other. They then looked forward at the boat and proceeded to board with Allodia.

The ship was a large beast of the sea. She was thick in width, medium in length, and tall. The center superstructure composed about four-stories from the deck and must have gone down at least three stories below. On the exterior, the upper-levels and railing were painted white while the lower levels were painted blue. The levels below the water were painted black. The superstructure was not creatively designed. The first three levels were a plain cube in shape with minimal porthole windows. The top-most deck, which must've been the bridge based on its design, was more creative in a hexagon shape and large windows on every available surface. There was a metal tower above the bridge that provided access to a tall pole extending upwards in the middle of the structure. Various technical equipment was also scattered along the roof. Towards the bow, on the side of the ship, was the ship's name: RV (research vessel) Ingstad.

The bow of the ship (front) had a folded crane over a small helipad platform. There were staircases on either side going up to the very top and very front of the ship, which also led to a thick circular pillar with a ladder going into the control room of the crane. The bridge of the ship stood out from the superstructure as it had large windows. Above the bridge was a sort of observation station with similar windows, but a vacant room with nothing but a table and stools. Above this station was an observation tower. Behind this tower was a large white sphere on stands and a sonar beacon spinning nearby.

Neither Diana nor Tristan had much time to look at further details of the ship as they rushed along behind Allodia, went up the boarding ramp and found themselves on the portside deck as Allodia went further some more to open a watertight door. She then led the kids into a corridor that ran along the perimeter of what appeared to be Deck A based on the imprint in the wall. Both of the walls were metallic, but they had a sophisticated and neat appearance that didn't give the interior a rustic and industrial appearance. On either side of the corridor were rail guards. Allodia held the door open for the kids to enter before closing it behind her.

"Woo, I think I might miss that bit of snow that was in Allabrese," Allodia remarked, pulling her hood back so that she could fix her hair. "I thought Charles said that you were staying home with Dr. Lambert. Don't you have school?"

"Bah, who cares about school? Am I right?" Tristan questioned.

"Tristan means that we do have school, but Charles thought that it would be more educational for us if we joined you guys."

"Oh, I suppose that's a good reason," Allodia admitted, looking at her before the two of them together, "but that doesn't explain what you were doing outside. Oh, Charlie, how could you be so irresponsible?"

Allodia shook her head.

"My brother said that he had two assistants coming around. I suppose he meant you then – there were only accommodations made for two others, so I suppose that must be true."

"Uh…" Tristan hesitated.

"Yes," Diana answered. "I guess you could call us that. Is that what he called us?"

"Tsk," Allodia replied. "All this time, I thought we were waiting for two additional people and not you two. We could have left sooner rather than later if he was just straightforward with me. Then again, that doesn't explain what you were doing in the rain…"

"We were lost," Diana explained. "One second we were with Charles, and the next we weren't. It's not his fault, but if we're all waiting for nothing, then I guess we could just leave and get this show on the road. Right?"

"Right," Allodia remarked, "well, sorry I wasn't around to greet him in person when he did arrive, or else I would have taken a bit more initiative. Regardless, welcome to the Research Vessel Ingstad. She's a fine craft and will be your home for the next week or so. We loaned her from the company for this mission – not that she was doing anything else. Anyways, let me take you to your rooms."

Allodia led the kids down the hall, going towards the stern before turning left again to enter what appeared to be a staff lounge on the left. It was a moderate room that extended from the corridor that cut through to the starboard corridor. It had armchairs, tables, coffee tables, vending machines, and even a bar in the corner with stools and taps. To the right were stairs that split left and right to more stairs that went to Deck B.

A crew member walked into the corridor between the stairs and the lounge. He was just about to pass Allodia when the four of them crossed paths.

"Kids, this is the first mate of the ship, Owen Gilkes," Allodia remarked to the kids as she presented a young man with black hair and thick eyebrows.

"Hello, nice to meet you," he said, shaking each of their hands.

"Owen, tell the captain that all crew are accounted for so that we can set off at once," Allodia said.

"Of course, Ms. Cabernet," Gilkes replied, nodding before going up the stairs and disappearing.

"We're currently running a crew of eleven including the captain and First Mate Gilkes, but don't worry, you won't have to get to know all of them unless you want to. It wouldn't hurt seeing that we'll be at sea with them for the next two weeks."

The three of them went upstairs to the next deck and entered a corridor that went down on either way before turning inwards. Allodia went to the very end, stopping at a watertight door at the end and stairs that went inwards and up to the next floor. Next to the stairs was an ordinary door with an ordinary doorknob. She brought her hand to the knob and turned it, pushing forward to enter a small and dark room. It was simple with two bunkbeds in each corner, desks in front of the beds and against the wall, and each desk with a chair and lamp. Between the two bunks at the opposite-end was a door that went into the bathroom.

"Diana, you can have this room. Since we're running such a small crew, there's plenty of room for everybody. The actual maximum occupancy for this ship is one-hundred people, with twenty-four rooms like this. The captain and first mate have their own privates rooms, of course, as well as the chief engineer and chief physician. We have a captain, a first mate, two engineers, a physician, two boatswains and four seamen. From the foundation, there's only myself and two others, and then there's you two, and Charlemagne."

"Wow, that's a lot of empty bedrooms," Tristan remarked. "So, we can have a room to ourselves then?"

"Yes, there's no need to share bedrooms this time around. When it comes to this mission, we only require the minimum amount of staff since the only real objective is to deliver cargo. Myself and the two other foundation members are here to lead that cause, while the boatswains and seamen will be offloading the cargo at our destinations."

"It'll feel a little lonely sharing a room with four beds by yourself," Diana pointed out.

"You know, you're absolutely right, Diana," Allodia remarked. "If you're feeling lonely, I wouldn't mind sharing a room with you. I'm sure Charles wouldn't mind the same, Tristan. In fact, his room is just past the shared bathroom ahead."

A single, but long signal of the horn emitted from outside. The three of them felt movement as the ship started to move.

"Anyways, I'll let you two get settled in for the time being. I'm sure you're both exhausted," Allodia said. "I'm going to fetch my things and bring them to this room so you don't feel so lonely, Diana. The level above us is the conference room, auditorium and cafeteria. Downstairs we have the lounge you saw, another conference room, a computer room and a gym. If you're feeling adventurous or bored, the engine room is downstairs, although the engineers might get angry at you. The cargo hold is also downstairs too. Try not to touch anything."

Allodia put her hand to the knob of the door as she prepared to leave the kids before turning to face them.

"Oh, and before you ask and before I forget, there is Wi-Fi… at least for now," she said. "If you don't have any questions, I'll go now."

"No, thanks, Allodia," Tristan replied, looking over to her.

"Alright, guys. I'm glad Charles decided to let you come along. I think this'll be a real nice experience for the two of you. I'll catch you later for lunch."

With her final words, Allodia closed the door behind her and let them get settled in. Tristan looked at Diana and crossed his arms.

"Assistants…" he said to her.

"What else was I supposed to say?" Diana replied. "No, 'We're here to smuggle ourselves onboard because we don't want to go to school and have a stupid bet about the artic?'"

"Charles is going to kill us for sure," Tristan remarked, sitting down on a bed. "We just got Allodia to ditch the real assistants that are supposed to help Charlemagne with his actual project."

"Forget them," Diana replied. "We're material enough to help Charles with whatever he's doing. Besides, you can't trust these interns – remember Johnny? All Charles is doing is looking for a couple of rocks – that's it. What could there be to do that's so advanced and he can't do on his own?"

"We're so dead," Tristan replied, shaking his head. "Why didn't you talk me out of this? I'm never letting you enable me like that again…"

"Oh, shush. You're to blame for this, not me," Diana said to him.

• •

"Hey, Charles," Allodia said, passing him in the corridor. "Just to let you know, I've set up the kids in their rooms. Tristan is going to share a room with you, and I'm going to share a room with Diana."

"Pardon?" Charlemagne responded, stopping and looking at her.

"Are you deaf?" Allodia questioned. "I said –"

"I heard what you said, and I'm confused. The children aren't with me – what kids are you talking about?"

"Yours," Allodia corrected. "Thanks for not telling me about them."

Charlemagne looked at his sister and slowly began to pick up his pace of breath. He formed a fist in his left hand and his eye twitched.

"Charlie?" Allodia questioned.

"Are you telling me…" Charlemagne said in a quiet tone, "that the children are here?"

"Yes, your 'assistants' are here and settled in," Allodia clarified.

"My what?!" Charlemagne shouted.

"Don't take that tone with me," Allodia scolded. "I found them outside in the pouring rain, completely lost. You told me that they weren't coming – you had me thinking that two scientists from the university were coming with you."

"They're not supposed to be here! My God... and the scientists... are they not here then? Please, tell me that this is some sort of crude joke on your part..."

"Is your memory failing you already?"

"My memory is fine," Charlemagne stated in a strict voice. "I'm telling you, I didn't bring the kids with me and they aren't my assistants. I wasn't being smart or trying to hide them as my 'assistants,' because I really did invite two interns from the University of Harlech. I left the kids in the hands of Judith – I know I did. God, is this all true?"

"Yes. Diana and Tristan are with us," Allodia replied, turning to face the ground and sigh."

Allodia then looked at her brother again.

"And I'm not turning this boat around at this point. We've delayed the trip as it is to bring you along, and I'm not delaying it anymore. We had just the right amount of fuel to make it to Point Alpha, and turning around will only set us back further."

"I knew it was strange when Ms. Piccard and Mr. Cook hadn't signed in with me before we left. I should have been more careful... I never could have predicted this..." Charlemagne muttered with a deep rage. "Where are they?"

"Calm down," Allodia replied. "If they haven't left their room, then that's where they'll be. Tristan is going to be sleeping with you in your room, and I'm sharing the room parallel with Diana."

"Oh, if they think they're coming with me to the arctic then they have something else planned for them. I'll send them back to Harlech for Ms. Quinn to retrieve them from the lifeboat I'll send them in," Charlemagne said, marching off to go to his room.

"Leave them alone!" Allodia shouted, rushing after him. "Just let them be!"

Charlemagne came around to the stairs and went up. He then went down the corridor towards his bedroom.

"Children!" Charlemagne shouted as he approached his room.

Charlemagne opened the door and didn't see anyone in his room. He then opened the bathroom door and then crossed to the other side. He knocked on the door beforehand, heard no response, and opened the door to see Tristan sat at the edge of the bed with Diana at the top bunk. She sat up and hid as Charlemagne looked at them with fury in his eyes. Tristan looked back at him with fright. He didn't say anything.

"Leave them alone," Allodia complained, catching up with Charles.

Charlemagne brought a hand to his head and then turned away from them.

"Good Lord, they're really here," he said in distress before turning back at them. "Why?!"

"Surprise?" Diana replied with a worried smile.

Act 2, Scene 3

Three days later, Diana and Tristan would resume their stay aboard the Ingstad with little options on Charlemagne's end. He thought about it as he worked in the conference room, converting it into a workshop for him to operate from. He had various maps open: tidal charts, ocean floor maps, water cycle maps, and his laptop running simulations.

The crackle of thunder rode into the darkened room where only the lights around the table were lit. It was dark outside despite being mid-noon. The boat was rocking back and forth with the torrential storm that thrived outside. The sound of waves splashing against the pothole windows could also be met occasionally if kept silent. Charlemagne got on without a care in the world, while others weren't so lucky.

Diana sat on a chair in her bedroom, hugging a waste bucket with her arms. She looked faint and ill. Her bedroom had set in with both Allodia and herself. On Diana's bunk was a messy top bunk with various small items next to her pillow including the same Holy Bible she had been reading since last spring. The book had a bookmark four-fifths of the way in. Tristan opened the bedroom door and stepped inside, putting down two pills on the desk before going to the bathroom to fetch a glass of water from an empty cup in his other hand.

"I never thought you'd be the one to get seasick," Tristan remarked, handing the glass to Diana before sitting down on the bunk below where Diana was sleeping.

"I'm not surprised I am," Diana replied, taking a pill and sipping the water.

Diana tilted her head back and swallowed it.

"I noticed when we go to school, I get nauseous if I keep my head down. It's why I don't read on the way to school anymore."

"Right," Tristan replied, standing up. "Well, that antiemetic will soothe your motion sickness for now. Why don't you come to the bridge with me? It could help you out too."

"Yeah, okay…" Diana replied in a weak voice, standing up and leaving the waste bucket on the desk. "Let's go."

Tristan took Diana's hand, helping her stand at ease as he brought arm around her waist. The two of them then exited the living quarters to make their way up the stairs to reach Deck C. Tristan held tightly to every available railing as they walked on.

From Deck C, all they needed was to walk up the stairs ahead of them to reach a short corridor that went down towards the bow before turning right. The two of them walked down and around, and at the end of the hall was a simple open door that led into the bridge. The kids went forward and entered it. It was quiet with various machines running on their own, and a single man sat up on a high-chair. It was Captain Neil Raleigh.

Both of them barely had the opportunity to see the sea captain, especially during the meals when everybody was in the cafeteria. He was an old man, about Charlemagne's size, but a bit shorter and bulkier. He had a thicker moustache and was completely bald. He wore a fleece cyan jacket over his white dress shirt. He simply looked forward and out the window as he made sure everything was fine on his own. He didn't even turn around or notice the kids entering.

The bridge had various technical machines and computers running. A map monitor displayed the location of the ship in the midst of the Bering Sea.

"Jesus Christ…" Tristan murmured as he looked out the window ahead.

The ship faced a wave as tall as the ship directly ahead of the bow. It loomed over them before they started to push over, climbing the wave to tilt the ship backwards before they came down to send them down, giving a kick in the stomach sensation that Diana felt every once in a while. Water splashed the windows of the bridge, causing automatic wipers to trigger and clear the glass for better vision. Ironically, it wasn't raining as the ship passed through a rough storm with rough waves, mighty gray clouds and harsh winds.

"Is it safe to be sailing in this storm?" Tristan asked as he walked Diana over to an empty seat.

"Oh, of course it is," the old man calmly replied in a west midland English accent, standing up from his seat as he looked down. "What the hell is he doing?"

"Huh?" Tristan questioned, looking away from Diana and walking over to look outside.

A man in a yellow poncho was at the bow, falling over occasionally due to the waves that hit the hull of the ship and splashed down atop of the man.

"I told him later... later," the old man said, walking over to a closet of the bridge. "Oh, you two kids stay here and keep an eye on the bridge. Everything's automated, so there shouldn't a problem. If there's a problem, sound the alarm and wake the first mate. I've got to tell this dumbass off..."

The old man took out a yellow poncho and was prepared to put it on when Tristan went over to him.

"Let me go," Tristan offered. "I can tell him."

The captain looked at Tristan, shrugged and then passed the poncho to him.

"Alright, but just be careful out there and stay close to the door. I don't need the two kids of Mr. Cabernet running overboard, so hurry along and be safe. If either of you fall over, you'll be gone for sure."

Diana frowned at those words, but didn't say anything. Tristan pulled the poncho down over himself and then looked to her.

"I'll be right back," he said to her before leaving.

"Tristan," Diana protested, standing up and walking over. "Tristan!"

Diana shouted from the top of the stairs, but Tristan ignored her. He made his way downstairs from deck to deck before reaching Deck A. He turned left at the main stairs, and then left again to go down to the watertight doors that led outside. Tristan started to turn the valve before the door opened up as he pushed forward.

"Just my luck," Tristan murmured.

The weather had worsened as it had started to rain. Tristan held tightly to the door frame as he eased himself out and looked over to the member of the ship crew that was tying down some cargo on the bow because the ropes had come loose.

"Hey," Tristan shouted, trying to get his attention. "Hey!"

It was no use. Tristan frowned and looked around. He looked down to the slippery ground and then over to the man as he continued to work in dangerous conditions. Tristan sighed. He looked around for places to hold on to so he could inch forward a little more. He stepped out and went to a pole with careful steps, trudging side to side with the force of the ship.

The boat started to climb up again, causing Tristan to feel gravity pushing him back as he stood on the wet surface of the bow. He quickly grabbed the pole ahead and held on for his life. Water splashed down at his face from the tip of the bow, but the man continued to work ahead.

"Hey!" Tristan shouted. "Get off the bow!"

The man paid no attention to him, especially as Tristan started to wave towards him.

"Is he deaf?" Tristan questioned himself. "GET OFF THE BOW!"

Nothing. The man continued to work. Tristan rolled his eyes and found his grip as he ship tilted down and reached smooth surfaces again momentarily. He looked at the distance between him and the seaman. It was less than ten meters. Tristan took a deep breath and let go of his embrace from the pole to start walking down, almost running to the man to tap him on the shoulder.

"What?" the man questioned in surprise, turning around and smacking Tristan in the face with his elbow.

Tristan felt the brute force of the smack across the cheek. It sent him backwards and onto the ground of the bow just as the ship started to tilt up and send a splash over the two of them.

"Oops," the man cried out in a foreign accent.

The splash rained down on them, but it wasn't the water that started to cause Tristan to slide down the deck with panicked and fearful eyes. He hit the side of the railing where he was stopped as the ship reached the crest of the wave. Tristan tried to pick himself up, but he couldn't bring himself forward without slipping onto his back. More panic filled him as he failed to attain a grip on the railings.

"Help!" Tristan shouted.

"I'm coming!" the man yelled from where he was.

Tristan looked forward as the ship started to descend, causing him to slide down now, but at a steep slope of the wave. The seaman held onto a rope he used as a safety rope as Tristan fell forward, sliding down to what appeared to be an inevitable fall into the stormy waters and sure death – waters that looked at him like predators to their prey. Suddenly though, before he could make his fall, he had arms around him as the ship stabilized at the trough.

The man helped him up and the two of them quickly went for the door where two other crew members had appeared with a life ring tied to some rope. One of the crew members took Tristan and the other, while the second pulled the door closed to stop any more water from entering in.

Tristan fell over on the ground with the man that had both put him in peril, but also saved him. The two had crash landed on the ground. The seaman that was out there was in fact the twenty-four year old Dane, Søren Kristiansen.

"What is wrong with you?" a boatswain questioned Søren.

"I was told to go out," Søren remarked. "You know that."

"After! After the storm!" the boatswain replied.

Tristan looked at either of the crew mates. The boatswain, Douglas Noble, who had short red hair underneath his grey beanie. Douglas' hair was unlike Tristan's hair, which was a combination of orange and blonde on brighter days and orange and brown on darker days. Douglas' hair was like Moira's in that it was saffron red. Although one couldn't see his hair due to his hat, he had a thick beard, fair skin, freckles, and light green eyes. The seaman with him was Drake Raleigh, the son of the sea captain. He had short light brown hair and a fair skin tone. Søren on the other hand had skin like Diana – extremely light with snow blonde hair atop his head and light blue eyes. He was very tall, perhaps six feet and four inches tall, and showed his youth.

"Are you alright, mate?" Drake asked, looking at Tristan.

Drake spoke in a west midland accent like his father.

"I'm shaken, but glad to be alive," Tristan replied.

"I was talking about the blood on your face," Drake responded.

"Huh?" Tristan questioned, bringing his hand to his face.

Tristan's face was not only wet with the saline water of the Pacific Ocean, but the salted blood that dripped from his nose.

"I didn't mean to hit you, Tristan. I'm sorry," Søren apologized, shaking his head. "It was an accident – believe me. You scared me."

"Don't worry about it," Drake replied.

"Yeah, it's just a little blood," Tristan added, removing the poncho.

Tristan looked forward and saw Diana and Dr. Vidkunsen turn up. The doctor had a first aid kit in hand and brushed past the kids to kneel down.

"Oh, Tristan, what happened?" Dr. Vidkunsen asked.

"Nothing," Tristan replied.

"A little accident, ma'am," Douglas explained.

Dr. Vidkunsen brought her hands to Tristan's cheeks. Her hands were cold. She looked at him and then opened up her first aid kit to retrieve some bandage cloth to wipe the blood from Tristan's face.

"Take a deep breath for me," the doctor asked, taking out a stethoscope and standing up.

The doctor went around to bring the diaphragm to Tristan's back. Tristan took a deep breath. Dr. Vidkunsen moved the stethoscope bell around his back as he kept taking deep breaths. She then went back to kneel in front of Tristan and bring a hand to his forehead. She then took her hands and brought them to his cheek again.

"You're cold," the doctor pointed out. "Can someone get a blanket for these boys?"

"Yes, doctor," the boatswain replied.

"Lean forward," Dr. Vidkunsen then asked of Tristan.

The doctor then brought her hand to the bridge of Tristan's nose.

"Any pain?"

"A little," Tristan replied.

"No fracture," the doctor remarked. "You're going to be okay."

The boatswain returned with two blankets. The doctor took one and brought it around Tristan.

"Stand up," Dr. Vidkunsen asked. "Diana, please take Tristan to his room to get warmed up. His nose will be fine."

"Thanks, doctor," Tristan replied, walking off with Diana.

"Come on, let's get you warm, dry and clean," Diana said, bringing and arm underneath the blanket to hold him.

Tristan was wet as if he had just gone swimming in his clothing, but Diana didn't mind.

"I'm sorry, Tristan," Søren said to him again. "I didn't mean to hit you. Please believe me."

"It's okay," Tristan replied. "I believe you, man. I forgive you."

Diana and Tristan walked off upstairs and went back to his room. They entered, passed through, and then entered the washroom where Diana sat Tristan down atop of the closed toilet. Tristan kept leaning forward with the cloth at his face.

"Pinch your nose," Diana instructed.

Tristan looked at her and removed the cloth from his face. He handed it to her, who took it and disposed of it. She then took a small towel and turned on the tap, leaving the water running for a bit. Tristan pinched his nose, causing Diana to roll her eyes.

"Keep the side of your index finger clamped down on your nose. Pinching it won't do anything. Use your finger to vice the clamp and add extra pressure.

Tristan didn't say anything and simply listened to her. The two of them looked at each other before Diana took the towel and brought it under the water. She then turned to face Tristan and got him to let go of his nose. Diana washed his face from the dried blood and then wiped downwards against each of

Tristan's cheeks. She then ran it over his forehead and brought a hand over his hair.

Diana and Tristan looked at each other silently. Tristan noticed that Diana's pupils were dilated and eyes focused on him.

"What is it?" Tristan asked in a congested voice.

"Nothing," Diana replied. "It's just – you're really handsome."

"Was I not handsome to you beforehand?"

"You know what I meant," Diana scolded, turning away from him to bring the towel into the sink.

Diana then looked at Tristan with a warm smile.

"Why don't you get out of those clothes, shower, and I'll get you some clean clothes?"

"Okay," Tristan replied, "but first let's just let this nosebleed clot out."

"Sure," Diana quietly said, nodding.

The two of them went quiet as Diana took care of the towel, squeezing it dry before setting it away from the sink and turning off the water.

"Are you still nauseous?" Tristan asked, looking over to her as he continued to clamp his nose.

"No, I think it's passed me a little with all the excitement just now," Diana replied, crossing her arms.

"How's that for another near-death experience?" Tristan remarked, rolling his eyes away from her. "I think that was scarier than hypothermia in Russia."

"Don't you just get to have *all* the near-death experiences during these adventures?" Diana said with a smile. "Although, I think Russia was by far the scarier experience for me."

"For you – I was out of my mind and unconscious for most of that. For this… it was like staring death in the face. Not even being on that alien ship was as scary as this with all that gunfire flying over my head and dead aliens at my feet – this adventure was supposed to be peaceful."

"You sound shaken up," Diana commented.

'Yeah, I am shaken up," Tristan replied, removing his hand from his nose. "I think I'm going to lie down for a moment after my shower."

Tristan stood up and walked over to the shower. He then turned around and looked at Diana.

"I just remembered – if we ever do get to the arctic, remind me to stay away from any unsteady ice. The last thing I think either of us want is a repeat of last time – I've had enough exhilaration, especially now, until next winter, I think."

"Will do," Diana replied, giving a warm smile.

Tristan started to remove his shirt.

"Thanks."

Act 2, Scene 4

"Ice! Approximately 20,000 meters ahead!" Drake shouted from the observation tower.

Diana and Tristan watched from the starboard railing as the ship continued to power on forward on the fifth day, rushing towards a thick layer of ice in the distance that neither of them could see from where they were. Tristan was even looking out through a pair of binoculars but could not see ahead by much.

"Where are we?" Diana asked Tristan.

"Chukchi Sea," Tristan answered

"Is that the arctic?"

"It's in the Arctic Ocean, so I'm going to say, yes."

The couple continued to look out to the horizon. The skies were a dark light blue and the sun was nowhere to be seen despite it being noon. There was a light stratus of clouds in the sky and it was approximately ten degrees below freezing.

"Alright, can we go back inside now? It's freezing out here," Diana complained.

"Sure, maybe I can get a better view of the ice from the bridge."

The two of them left the company of the railing and made their way back towards a flood gate going into the ship. From there, they took the stairs upwards to the bridge where Captain Raleigh was stood by the console with a phone at his ear.

Tristan walked up to the window and brought up his binoculars to his eyes. He looked out and could see a thick layer of ice in the far distance, stretching in either direction. The entire surface of the ice was smooth.

Captain Raleigh slammed the telephone into the console and then went to a panel as he brought a switch down. The sea captain then picked up the telephone again and started to turn a dial before bringing it to his ear.

"Come on, pick up…" the sea captain complained.

"What's up?" Tristan asked, looking at him.

"Bloody engineer isn't picking up his damn phone," the sea captain explained. "We're approximately twenty kilometers from that sheet of ice, and he's not confirming my directions on the telegraph. If we don't slow down before we get to that ice, it could be bad news for all of us."

"Is the engineer sleeping?" Tristan then asked.

"He shouldn't be," the captain replied, slamming the phone down again. "Him and his apprentice are supposed to be rotating between nights and days, and monitoring from the control room. He's obviously stepped out for whatever reason."

"Oh…"

"Look, can you two do me a favor and go down to the engine room to alert the engineer?"

"Sure thing, but how do we get to the engine room?" Tristan asked.

"There's a door around the back of Deck A that should let you down to the control room. From there, be sure to put on any personal protective equipment you can find before entering the engine room to find that deaf oaf."

"Alright, and what do we tell him?"

"To slow the bloody ship down before we hit that ice," Raleigh replied. "Now go – we haven't got a second to lose!"

"Aye aye, captain," Tristan responded, turning to Diana. "Come on, let's go."

The couple went back to the stairs and took them all the way down to Deck A again. From there, they walked down the hall to reach the rear of the deck where they were brought to a hallway extending from starboard to port. On the portside, there was a heavy-duty door that read, 'Engine Room' and below this, 'Authorized personnel only.'

Tristan walked up to the door with Diana and brought his hand around the doorknob. The door was unlocked and opened for them to look down at the step ladder going into the bowels of the stern of the ship. The couple took careful steps going down to a vestibule with lockers on the left side and a bench on the right side. In front of them was a door with a window in the middle looking into a control room. Tristan opened the door and stepped inside.

The control room was similar to the bridge in that it had a large glass window looking downwards, but instead of looking out to sea, the window looked down to a room lit by orange lights with various machines and machinery around. Behind the glass window were an assortment of meters and monitors with all sorts of different measurements and options. At the top of one of the monitors displayed three different numbers measured by rotations per minute (rpm).

Of course, the control room was empty. A telephone by a panel similar to the one in the bridge that the sea captain was touching was ringing. Tristan walked over to the phone and picked it up.

"Hello?" Tristan answered.

"Hello? Gus?" the sea captain questioned.

"No, Tristan. The engineer isn't here."

"In that case, he must be in the engine room. Be careful in there and hurry up!"

The sea captain hung up and left Tristan looking over to Diana. Diana was looking to the rest of the room. On the opposite wall from the large glass window were a series of four grey cabinet-like devices with meters in the middle of them and various dials and lights. At the end of the room was a door going into the engine room.

"Alright, let's get going," Tristan said, walking over to the door.

Tristan turned the knob and was met by an instant burst of heat and sound. He then closed the door and looked down at the sign below the window of the door. It displayed a warning to put on personal protective equipment before entering. Tristan looked around for some earmuffs and found some on a rack.

"Wait," Diana said, standing next to a door adjacent to the door going into the engine room. "Maybe we should just wake the other engineer?"

"No way," Tristan replied, pointing at the sign on the door. "It says 'Do not disturb.' The last thing you want to do is to disturb an engineer. Come on, let's put on some ear protection and then go in looking for this dude."

Diana fetched one for herself and then gave another to Tristan. The couple then removed their parka jackets before going to the door. Tristan opened it and stepped out into the engine room where it was hot and humid.

The engine room was a tall room going all the way down to the bottom of the boat. In other words, it was about two stories tall with the control room being at the top of the room and the kids on a metal-grated balcony near another step-ladder going down into the depths of the room. At the bottom of the room, in the middle, was a large engine – a monstrous machine with four step ladders going upwards to platforms on the right side and a large grey diesel tank on the left side. The space around the main engine was crowded with additional devices around this main piece. In front of the main engine, going towards the bow, were four tall devices. They were also long. The engineer was nowhere to be found in this part of the engine room.

"Look," Tristan said, pointing to another staircase to go deeper.

Diana could not hear him, so he went over to tap her on the shoulder before pointing at the step ladder he had found. The two then went down to the third sublevel where the main engine extended as a single casket in an arc angle. At one of the corners was a large gear turning. The duo walked around the engine towards the stern and saw a thick shaft that protruded from the middle rear of the engine. The shaft went towards the stern behind a grate. It also spun and appeared to be greasy.

Behind the couple were more machines going along and deeper into the boat. They started to walk along this corridor, which had a low ceiling. It was warmer and more humid in this space. They walked around with caution and came to a junction. There, observing some valves with a flashlight was the engineer. Diana tapped Tristan's shoulder and the two then went over to him.

"Hey!" Tristan shouted, but it was no use as the engineer wore a hardhat and ear muffs.

Tristan rolled his eyes and took a deep breath. He looked at the engineer, who had fair skin, grey hair and a thick moustache over his lips. He was taller than the sea captain and wore a dark green jumpsuits, which was dirtied with oil stains.

"I'm not getting hit in the head again because somebody can't hear me," Tristan muttered to himself.

Tristan timidly walked towards the man, patted him on the arm and then stepped back. The man jumped as he turned at the kids. His face then turned red with anger as he started to yell, but neither of them could hear him. Tristan instead simply began to point at him and then back out into the corridor. He then started to leave with Diana, hoping he would follow, but he wouldn't. Tristan became more aggressive with hand signals before going to the man, tugging at his jumpsuit to get him to follow them back upstairs.

Once inside the control room, Tristan and Diana removed their ear protection and left them on a table. The engineer followed them inside, removed his hardhat and ear protectors and then looked at the kids.

"What the hell do you kids think you're doing in my engine room?" the man said in a strict voice.

"Shut up," Diana replied, annoyed at him.

The chief engineer jerked his head back in shock over Diana's rudeness.

"The sea captain's been trying to contact you and it's urgent. We're approaching ice and he needs you to slow the ship down," Diana explained.

"Oh..." the engineer replied, looking over to the control panel. "How far are we?"

"About twenty kilometers, but this was about five to ten minutes ago..."

"Really?" the man replied, pausing for a moment before picking up a phone. "We don't have that much time then."

The man turned a dial on the phone and brought it to his ear.

"Mhm..." the chief engineer affirmed. "Yeah."

The engineer then brought the phone down and went to the telegraph, which was a switch with three options up and down. The man started to bring it down from where it was previously at the top most option. Tristan watched.

"What's he doing?" Diana asked Tristan.

Tristan didn't reply.

"I'm slowing the boat down," the chief engineer instead replied. "Do you know how you slow a boat down without any brakes?"

Tristan shrugged. Neither of them replied.

"You reverse the direction of the propeller until it loses momentum, then you keep it on slow," the chief engineer explained. "Of course, I didn't expect either of you to know that."

The engineer kept his eyes on a monitor as the kids simply stood behind him at the other side of the room and watched him. After a couple of minutes had passed, the engineer brought the switch up to the first option beyond the middle option.

"There we go – that should settle us," the chief engineer simply said before turning to the kids. "It's a good thing too – we would have slid over that ice, and the ship possibly have fallen over. Thanks for letting me know."

"Yeah..." Tristan responded.

"Okay... well, if there's anything else you need, you can go now," the chief engineer said to them.

Tristan looked at Diana before they took their coats and went upstairs again.

"And don't let me catch you two down here again!" the engineer remarked as they left.

The duo walked back up to Deck A and closed the door behind them. Tristan then looked at Diana as they made the same face, agreeing that their encounter with the engineer was both awkward and strange. They then walked back down the corridor towards the stairs going to the bridge and went up to join the sea captain.

The ice was closer than it previously was and vaster. The ship was about a kilometer away from it. The two watched as they slowly made their approach towards it.

"Is slowing down the ship all there is to it?" Tristan asked the captain.

"Oh, yeah," the captain replied. "You'll see it when we reach it, but there's really nothing else to it."

Tristan continued to watch the ice in anticipation as they started to reach the ice. The ship went straight forward and started to slide up, raising them slightly before the weight of the boat came crushing down on the ice. The ship continued this way as they continued onwards.

"Wow," Tristan remarked. "I didn't think it would be like that."

"So, we're just navigating over the ice then?" Diana asked.

"Head on over to the stern of the ship and find out for yourselves," the sea captain suggested.

The two then went downstairs to Deck C to go along to the stern of the boat. They came out to a balcony that looked over to a large helipad with a giant 'H' marked atop along the most posterior portion of Deck A. On the helipad was a cargo helicopter parked with a tarmac covering the double rotors.

Tristan and Diana walked down a staircase to come onto the helipad and then went right to the back of the boat to look behind the ship where a trail of open water was being left behind in the path of the ship. The two of them brought their hands to the railing and simply watched the boat carry on, leaving its trail in the ice. Tristan looked below to a balcony below and then to the side to some stairs. He took Diana to the stairs so that they could get closer to the water.

"You know, this is nice," Diana remarked, looking at Tristan. "Aside from you almost falling into the ocean, this is turning into a really nice vacation – it's peaceful, and we needed that after what we went through in the summer."

Tristan smiled at her and the couple held hands. Once they were finished admiring the work of the icebreaker, they started to walk around the railing and come along a corridor where the lifeboats were stored. At the end of the exterior corridor, they entered back into the boat.

••

Charlemagne continued to study maps in his makeshift workshop before looking over to the door as the kids came to visit him. He looked over to them, straightened up, and then looked back down at his map.

"Any progress?" Tristan asked, walking in with Diana.

"Actually, I have made some," Charlemagne answered. "I've been tracking the different meteorites that have fallen into the Arctic Ocean, and have followed one in particular, which should have floated into a fjord on the northern coast of Greenland."

Charlemagne pointed to a large map of the Arctic Circle and near the northern coast of Greenland. He then traced his finger down towards a fjord.

"However, this fjord leads into a subterranean cavern, or grotto, which means that it'll have trapped itself inside this cave as though it were a net. I've been sure to double-check my research, but I'm certain that what I've deduced is factual."

"How are we going to get it?" Tristan asked.

"Well, the only way we can – at this time of the year, most of the entire Arctic is frozen over with ice, which means we'll have to travel under this ice and go into this cave to collect the rock. We are going to have to travel by submarine."

"Cool, but we don't have a submarine," Tristan pointed out.

"No, which is why I'm going to have to get into contact with the right people to have a research submarine airlifted to Checkpoint Alpha before we get there. It'll cost a lot of money but will be worth it in the end."

Act 3, Scene 1

Checkpoint Alpha stood in the distance, surrounded by clear water with broken pieces of ice floating around. The skies were dark around and there were bright lights shining from the port town's various portable homes. The lights were brightest by the actual harbor where they shined down on the concrete docks like a sports stadium.

The RV Ingstad slowly made its approach to the town and parked along the docks. From there, various workers started to roam around with forklifts by the portside of the bow. Diana and Tristan watched from the railing with Allodia and Charlemagne. It was now late into day six on their journey, and they were at the top of the Yukon at their first stop before venturing towards the various remote settlements on the many islands of the Northwest Territories, Nunavut territory, and then Greenland.

"This is nothing like how I expected the arctic to be," Diana said to Tristan as she looked out to Checkpoint Alpha.

"I told you," Tristan responded, "but don't be so hasty. We haven't seen the core of the arctic yet."

A metal rail was brought up so that Charlemagne, Allodia and the kids could disembark and go down to the dock and leave the boat for a moment. Tristan looked behind him as he saw the doors of the cargo hold of the RV Ingstad open, revealing the mass of cargo inside. He stopped with Diana to look as forklifts entered and started to load palettes of cargo onto the forks and left them out.

The nightshift crew of the Ingstad were busy at work, led by Boatswain Adrian Hawkins, a tall man with fair skin, short light brown hair and blue eyes. He looked to be in his thirties. He led Seaman Hurley Darwin and Dylan Jones. Darwin was an older gentleman with a thick white beard and long hair. He looked like your typical stereotypical sea captain, but he wasn't a sea captain. His compatriot, Jones, was younger, but still rugged looking with dark brown hair, an unshaven face and medium length hair. They both looked like miserable men. Each of them were dressed in overalls like fishermen and had thick jackets over their backs.

Tristan watched for another second before catching up with Charlemagne as they went over to a hangar where there was a pickup truck with a platform behind it holding a small submarine about ten feet tall and twelve feet long It was yellow in color and had small windows on the side. In the front was a large transparent sphere with two seats side by side at the front and an additional seat in the back. Around the front of the bubble was a frame with lanterns pointing forward and diagonally away from the bubble. In addition, from underneath the bubble, the boat had two arms that extended out with clamps at the end of them. There was clear black print on either side that clearly stated its name, 'SRV Voyager.'

Allodia was with Charlemagne as they looked at the vessel and Charlemagne signed some papers for the item.

"How much money did you spend bringing this in when you could have spent that same money bringing in more supplies?" Allodia questioned with a frown.

"The trouble there is that there's no more room for supplies on the Ingstad," Charlemagne pointed out. "The submarine is going to sit atop of the bow of the ship. There's nowhere else to put it."

Charlemagne returned a clipboard back to a man and then pointed over to the boat. The man took the clipboard and got into the pickup truck, starting the engine and driving the platform over near the bow of the ship as workers were still taking out supplies. The platform was left near the boat where the four of them simply waited as the unloading was completed. Once all the necessary cargo was unloaded, the workers began to load palettes with items that wasn't meant to be off-loaded, but were simply in the way, and items that were brought to this port for them to pick up.

"There's no reason for you children to be awake this late," Charlemagne reasoned to the kids. "There's nothing to watch here."

"I'm interested," Tristan replied. "All of this is better than sitting around in my room being bored."

"Yeah, besides, it's not like we'll be missing out on any daylight by sleeping in. I haven't seen the sun in almost three days."

"Nor will you be seeing the sun until the new year, probably. I've greatly mistaken how long we'd be out at sea, and it appears like we won't be turning around until Christmas Day."

"I specifically told you that this was a round-trip 10,000 kilometer voyage," Allodia strictly said. "It was going to take at most, like, three weeks."

The forklifts began to exit the cargo hold of the Ingstad and venture off into the port. Meanwhile, the crane atop of the bow of the ship began to move around. Tristan could see the boatswain controlling the crane and lowering the wire towards the submarine. The worker got out of his pickup truck and went around to properly hook the crane to the tether around the submarine.

"Ready!" the man yelled before hopping off.

Once he was off, the crane began to lift the submarine up from the platform and bring it towards a platform on the bow. The seamen proceeded to tie the submarine down on the platform, fastening it in case of any unsteady movements, including the icebreaking. The pickup truck disappeared in front of them, and with no more work to be done, the four of them started to make their way back to the ramp to walk back onto the ship.

The boatswain came around to detach the ramp. The ramp was brought away from the ship and additional workers near the stern unmoored the ship. Tristan then looked over to the submarine where it sat on the helipad platform on the bow of the ship.

"Come along now, children," Charlemagne stated. "It's nearly one o'clock and time to go to bed even if we're in polar night."

Charlemagne, Allodia, and the kids walked back into the boat, but stopped by the ship lounge. There was a quiet sound of music playing in the background as somebody had left the jukebox on. Charlemagne turned to the kids.

"The submarine I've requested has space for two additional people in addition to myself, who will be piloting the vessel," Charlemagne explained. "The two of you cost me my additional help by coming along and stranding those poor folk in Harlech, but instead of forcing you to come with me and help me as punishment, I am instead going to ask you of your preference: would you rather come with me and journey under the arctic waters or stay here aboard the ship and venture to the various settlements with Allodia?"

"Wow, now you decide to ask us," Tristan remarked.

Charlemagne frowned at him.

"I mean, I would love to hop aboard your submarine," Tristan corrected himself.

"Yeah, that sounds fun," Diana replied. "No offense, Allodia."

"Very well," Charlemagne responded. "I'll make preparations that we have enough supplies for the three of us. I must warn you, it might not be as exciting as you expect it to be. It still surprises me that the two of you went to this great length to become stowaways, but I suppose neither of you expected the journey to turn out like this – to be uneventful. I told you that it was purely a research mission. Likewise, submerging into the depths of the arctic won't be any more exciting than being on the Ingstad has been. Are you sure you wish to come with me?"

"I'm positive," Tristan replied. "A change of scenery is nice."

"Yeah, besides, we're going to be on this boat for the journey back, right?"

Charlemagne nodded before turning to Allodia. Allodia shrugged.

"If that's what the kids want to do, then I'm okay with it," Allodia said.

"It's settled then," Charlemagne responded. "The two of you will come with into the depths of the Arctic Ocean to find this meteorite."

Act 3, Scene 2

Charlemagne set down a container on the bow of the ship. It was one of about five containers he had prepared to take with him onto the submarine. Tristan stood nearby, alone with Charlemagne, who began to pass him the containers to bring up to the platform.

On their ninth day, they were at the top of the country and had just left Alert, Nunavut earlier in the morning. The Ingstad was now making its way down between Ellesmere Island and the coast of Greenland. It was mid-noon, but twilight dark outside with a light snow falling down.

Tristan helped bring each container, each weighing approximately fifty pounds each to the platform. From there, Charlemagne had Tristan climb up to the top of the submarine where he found two doors with valves to enter the submarine. The first was atop of the transparent sphere and provided direct entry into the cockpit, and the second was further back and wider. Tristan helped Charlemagne up onto the top of the submarine for him to go and open the larger valve, which led into a small airlock with another valve door. The chute into the base of the submarine offered a small ladder, which Charlemagne climbed down.

Tristan walked over and looked down into the darkness of the submarine. Charlemagne then reappeared and looked up to Tristan.

"Right now, I believe there'll be enough space here for our supplies," Charlemagne said, climbing out of the submarine. "I'll lift the boxes up, and you take them. I'll then climb up and take them from you again as you lower them to me into the vessel."

"Sure thing," Tristan replied.

Charlemagne looked down at the platform and felt uneasy about jumping. He then looked around to the side and saw a ladder for him to climb down. From there, he went over to the first box, lifted it up and brought it to Tristan to pull onto the top of the submarine. They did this with each of the box before Charlemagne climbed up the side ladder and went down into the boat.

Tristan took each box and then lowered them into the boat for Charlemagne to sort. He then came out of the submarine and looked over to Tristan.

"Alright, now that we have that sorted, it's time to go get our things and tell the crew that we'll be needing their help to lower us into the water," Charlemagne explained.

Charlemagne then climbed out and climbed down the side ladder with Tristan. The two walked back into the Ingstad and went to their room. Tristan had prepared his backpack last night and pulled it up to bring around himself. He then opened the bathroom door and walked into Allodia and Diana's room.

Allodia was at her desk with her laptop open. She wore glasses as she read the screen on her laptop. She turned to Tristan who was looking over to Diana, finishing packing her own backpack. Diana had her camera, which Charlemagne gifted to her as an early birthday present last summer, around her neck on a strap.

"Ready?" Tristan asked her.

"Yeah, let's go," Diana replied, bringing her own backpack around herself.

Diana turned to Allodia.

"See you," Diana said.

Allodia waved goodbye and then stood up. She followed the kids into Charlemagne and Tristan's room.

Charlemagne had brought his own backpack around himself and looked over to Allodia as she brought the kids over.

"Be safe down there," Allodia cautioned. "I hope you find what you're looking for."

"Thank you," Charlemagne responded. "We'll be back and in contact with Captain Raleigh. Hopefully we won't venture too far and neither will you."

"Don't worry, we'll be in the neighborhood. We have several islands to visit."

Charlemagne nodded and then left the bedroom with the kids. They walked down the corridor and went all the way down to Deck A. They then exited the superstructure and came outside again where the boat crew were busy untethering the submarine. Drake Raleigh approached Charlemagne with a radio in his hand.

"My father told me to give this to you," Drake said, handing him a handheld radio. "It's a long-range satellite radio to call us in the case of a medical emergency."

"Thank you," Charlemagne responded, taking the radio and clipping it to his belt with the radio clip.

Charlemagne shook Drake's hand before the seaman went off to help the boat crew. Diana followed Tristan and Charlemagne up the steps to the platform where they then climbed up. Instead of entering through the airlock, they simply entered through the bubble to hop down, one by one with Charlemagne being last of the two. Diana moved into the rear of the submarine, which was dark with small pothole windows. The containers Tristan and Charlemagne were moving earlier were positioned along the back and there was enough space to stretch out two sleeping bags side-by-side.

Tristan sat down in the seat next to the pilot seat. He then took off his backpack and left it next to him. He held a smile on his face as he got comfortable before turning to Charlemagne who was communicating with the boat crew. He was giving them a thumbs up before closing the hatch. He then went down to the pilot seat and began to fumble around with the controls as well as adjust the seat.

"Do you even know how to drive a submarine?" Tristan asked

"I looked at the manual beforehand and have a brief idea," Charlemagne responded. "There's not much to it."

Charlemagne picked up a headset and brought it over his ears. There was also a headset for Tristan to pick up. He did so and put it over his head and ears. Charlemagne began to start the engine of the submarine and turn on the panel next to him. He adjusted the radio set to a certain frequency before pressing into his mic to speak.

"Voyager to Ingstad, radio check," Charlemagne spoke.

There was a brief pause.

"We read you, Voyager," Captain Raleigh replied.

"Copy that," Charlemagne answered. "We're deploying in about five-mikes."

"Copy that."

Diana came around to the seat behind the pilot seat. She then sat down and left her stuff next to her, which was also next to where Charlemagne had left his things.

The crane began to slowly lift them up from the platform. Tristan looked out to the ice next to them, which stretched on for miles. However, they were in a clear patch away from the main body of ice, and the icebreaker was currently not chopping through a path. The ship was still moving as they were preparing to drop them overboard. The submarine swung around as the crane lifted them and then started to bring them around to the side. The arm of the crane then extended forward so that the submarine was now hovering over the ocean waters.

The tether slowly began to lower them into the water. Tristan could look down at his feet and through the bubble as they got closer to the surface. The crane then stopped with about a feet of distance between the craft and the ocean. Then, they dropped.

The submarine made its impact against the ocean and floated up and down before settling. Tristan and Diana held on as Charlemagne fumbled around with controls. Water hit against the spherical dome, but all was okay as they simply floated on the surface.

"I'm going to blow air from the balusters, which will let us sink downwards," Charlemagne said.

Charlemagne hit a switch, which caused the ship to start to sink. The water hitting the spherical dome got higher and higher until the entirety of the sphere was under the sea. The submarine continued to plummet downwards into the darkness of the depths of the ocean. Charlemagne turned on the lanterns around, which provided minimal light around them.

"How deep can we go?" Tristan asked as they continued to sink downwards.

"The vessel can withstand a maximum of one-hundred atmospheres of pressure, so about 1,000 meters of depth, which is just shy of the average depth of the arctic," Charlemagne responded, monitoring their depth. "At present, we're only a couple of meters down. I need us to be at least a hundred meters before we start to move forward towards the coast of Greenland. We won't be travelling any faster than the Ingstad under the water, unfortunately, as the diesel engine on this machine cannot go faster than five knots."

Charlemagne continued to monitor their depths before reversing the switch he used to blow air from the balusters.

"In order to reach zero buoyancy, I have to release just the right amount of water," Charlemagne explained.

"Just like in space," Tristan muttered.

"That's right."

Charlemagne finished manipulating the vessel before putting both hands on the controls. He went to another panel and started to press some buttons that caused the back of the ship to hum. Diana looked behind at the darkness before she continued to look out and around her. The water was black and there was nothing to see around them. The ocean was devoid.

"I think I'm starting to regret picking this option," Diana remarked.

"Why?" Tristan asked, looking around. "We're underwater!"

"It's creepy down here – what if one of us has to use the washroom or something?"

"There are urinals in one of the containers I packed," Charlemagne replied. "You can seek privacy in the observation chamber. A substance in the urinal will cause urine and feces to turn into a gel that doesn't smell."

"You see – everything is sorted. We have enough food, and hopefully, enough urinals to last us the rest of the day," Tristan said to her.

Diana crossed her arms as she sat back in her chair. She then uncrossed her arms and opened her backpack to take out her Bible and start to read.

Tristan in the meanwhile was focused on what Charlemagne was doing. The submarine had started to move forward. A panel between Charlemagne and Tristan, above the radio, was a GPS map with coordinates for them to follow. Tristan looked out of the bubble and saw a small group of fish swim past them. He smiled and then continued to focus ahead as they started to move forward in their journey.

Act 3, Scene 3

A couple of hours had passed as the submarine went forward into the darkness. According to the GPS, they were less than a kilometer away from the coast of Greenland, but still deep underwater. Diana was deep in her book and had lost attention to the exterior and the cockpit kept quiet with no chatter between the three of them. Tristan had quickly grown bored of the exterior as well, which displayed an endless nothingness in the great aquatic void around them. Charlemagne was focused on maintaining the right path to the fjord.

Diana closed her book and began to stretch her arms. She gave a loud yawn and looked forward at the nothingness outside. She then looked down to Tristan and Charlemagne.

"Does anybody know what time it is?" Diana questioned.

Tristan took out his phone and looked at the time.

"About a quarter to nine," Tristan answered. "Why?"

"I'm getting sleepy – are we almost there?"

"Almost," Charlemagne simply replied.

"Okay..." I'm going to go and set up my sleeping bag for some sleep then," Diana said, removing her seatbelt and climbing into the back of the sub.

"Goodnight," Tristan simply said.

Diana opened one of the containers and took out a sleeping bag. She then stretched it out and started to remove her jacket. It was slightly cold in the submarine, but not as cold as it was outside in the water or on the surface. However, it was still cold enough that Diana could see her breath. She set up her jacket to use as a pillow and then got into the sleeping bag. She brought her head against the makeshift pillow and looked out into the darkened waters through one of the portholes.

The water was eerily black. She continued to look out at the water until her eyes closed as if on their own. They then opened and opened wide as she thought she had seen something pass upwards by the window. She blinked several times and then stood up. Diana looked over to the boys, but they were unstimulated by anything. Nervous, Diana simply sat where she was and decided to look over to the next porthole where it was as dark as the one on her left. She then looked over to Charlemagne.

"Uh… hey, Charles?" Diana said.

"What is it, Diana?" Charlemagne responded.

"I have just a general question – what kind of wildlife should we be able to spot around here?"

"Plenty of wildlife from the smallest of planktons to the largest of whales – do you have anything more specific?"

"Yes, the large kind," Diana replied.

"Well, there should be narwhals, which I'm surprised we haven't seen. A certain kind of jellyfish should also be very common. And then there are seals and walruses."

"Any type of sea animal we should be particularly worried of?" Diana then asked.

Charlemagne paused for a moment.

"Not at the top of my mind. No," Charlemagne answered.

"I think I saw something out there," Diana confessed. "It was big and red – red like a lobster."

"What?" Charlemagne questioned. "I don't know what you saw."

Tristan looked behind to Diana. He saw a look of genuine fear on her face.

"Look!" Diana shouted, pointing forward.

Tristan turned around as he saw the tentacles of a large creature pass them and go left. Tristan's eyes widened and he attempted to look left to see what it was. He then looked at Charlemagne.

"Did you see what that was?" Tristan asked.

"Yes," Charlemagne responded with a similar look of fright.

"What are we going to do?" Tristan then asked. "What if it comes back?"

"Hopefully, it won't dare to attack us," Charlemagne responded. "It shouldn't. Look, we're almost at the fjord and will be safe in shallow waters."

The ship motioned sideways to the right in a moment of brute force. A siren sounded from the cockpit, which caused Diana to worry more as she looked around.

"Damn," Charlemagne remarked, holding the steering wheel with tight fists as he attempted to regain control.

Tristan then looked upwards as the saw tentacles launch themselves onto the sphere of the cockpit, pressing down and blocking their view. A second alarm went off from the cockpit and the ship began to submerge deeper into the water.

"Oh no," Charlemagne remarked. "We're building pressure – it's making us go deeper!"

"Do something!" Diana shouted.

Charlemagne began to panic as he looked around at the controls. Tristan simply kept his eyes up at the tentacles of the beast. Diana could see more tentacles attaching its suckers to the portholes on either side. Tristan then looked to the controls where he saw their depth increase from five-hundred meters to six-hundred meters, to seven-hundred meters, and then eight-hundred meters.

"Charles…" Tristan said, "we're not going to survive below one-thousand meters."

"I know," Charlemagne shouted, "just give me a moment!"

The ship shook as they hit the bottom of the ocean at almost nine-hundred meters. Tristan could see the white ground around them. Meanwhile, Charlemagne fumbled with a joystick and then hit a button. The lights of the ship flickered as well as the panels. The suckers of the tentacles let go and the creatures floated off, forward in the direction they were going towards.

"What did you do?" Diana asked.

"I brought one of the arms towards the creature and gave it a mild electrical shock," Charlemagne responded, removing his seatbelt.

"It's coming back!" Tristan observed aloud.

"Hold on a moment," Charlemagne replied, going into the rear chamber and towards one of the containers.

Charlemagne fumbled around with their food and took out some cans of tuna as well as a can opener.

"Help me open these," Charlemagne said, giving Diana a can opener.

The two began to quickly open cans, spilling fishy juices onto the ground in their haste. Once they had about five open, Charlemagne went over to the larger hatch and opened it gently.

"Pass me those cans," Charlemagne said.

Diana passed them to him and he began to load them atop of the hatch door before bringing it up and securing it. Tristan watched as the giant squid flew past them on the right and then the left. Charlemagne returned to the cockpit and found an emergency release for the rear hatch. He hit it and then took control of the steering panel so they could go forward.

Once they were a couple of meters forward, Charlemagne released water from the balusters so they could float up a considerable height – to about one-hundred meters in depth. He then began to take them towards the shallow coast of Greenland.

Tristan held his breath for a minute, but it had passed. The giant squid had left them alone with the bait. Tristan relaxed in his chair for another minute before removing his seatbelt so that he could go and lie down in the back. Diana was still sitting in her sleeping bag, looking out to the water, expecting the squid to return, but it didn't.

"Are you okay?" Tristan asked her.

"Yeah, I'm okay – we weren't eaten by a giant squid, so I can't complain too much."

"We're almost there," Charlemagne instead said to them. "We're just coming into the fjord now. Approximately another five minutes before we enter the cave."

"Good," Tristan replied.

"Yes, that creature won't harass us from shallow waters, so we should be safe."

Tristan returned to his seat and sat down. He looked up and could see the bottom of the ice. They were very close to it. The surface wasn't as smooth as he expected it to be, but bumpy.

The Voyager continued forward as they met the rocky entrance of a cavern into the coast. The submarine was just small enough for them to pass through without hitting any of the edges. Tristan observed the rocky edges of either side. The rock was a dark green as if it had a slimy algae growing overtop. They continued along into the cave for approximately another five minutes before Tristan observed above them that the water was not iced over and they could rise. In addition, they had run to the end of the cavern and met a rocky wall.

Charlemagne released more water from the balusters and gently raised them out of the water. He stopped when they had a clear vision of the ceiling of the cave from the top of the spherical bubble of the cockpit. Both of the boys observed that they had about another five meters of height, so Charlemagne continued to raise them up and out of the water.

The submarine floated in the small pool of the cavern with its lights providing light into the narrow tunnel ahead of them. Tristan and Charlemagne looked around ahead at the rocky surroundings, especially for a meteorite, but there was nothing. Charlemagne attempted to bring the side of the submarine closer to the coastline before he brought the engine of the submarine to a halt. Charlemagne then turned to Tristan.

"We're here," Charlemagne said to him.

Charlemagne got out of his seat and went up to open the hatch of the cockpit. He then climbed out and looked around the cavern.

The entrance was small and the floor was smooth and led up a couple of steps to go deeper through a tunnel ahead. Charlemagne jumped off from the boat and then started to say something to Tristan, but he couldn't hear him. Tristan got out from his seat and poked his head up through the open hatch.

"What?" Tristan asked him.

"Fetch some rope from one of the containers," Charlemagne directed. "I'll moor the submarine to this rock over here and set up a fire."

Tristan brought his head down and looked over to Diana who was putting her coat on. Tristan took out some rope and went back over to toss it to Charlemagne. Charlemagne tied one end to a stalagmite while Tristan tied the other to the submarine. Diana then brought her head out from the cockpit and looked around at the cave. She then climbed out and went over to the surface to be with Charlemagne. Tristan went back down to get some supplies and came up with some firewood and flint. He crossed over onto the surface of the boat and proceeded to help

Charlemagne light a fire on the damp surface of the cave, which gave them instant warmth.

Charlemagne brought a sleeping bag out and laid it down next to the fire. Diana and Tristan returned to the submarine to get their own sleeping bags and lay them nearby the fire. Tristan looked over to Charlemagne who was observing the ceiling of the cave with a flashlight. He was tracing the path of the smoke to see where it was going. It was going deeper into the cave. He then returned to the fire and sat down atop of his sleeping bag.

"We'll get some sleep here and then in about eight hours' time, we'll go spelunking into the depths of the cave," Charlemagne said. "Get some rest for now – we had a long day."

"Sure thing," Tristan replied, laying down in his sleeping bag and looking up to the ceiling.

The reflection of the water shined against the ceiling thanks to the fire. He continued to look upwards before turning onto his side. Tristan looked over to Diana in the sleeping bag next to him. The two then fell asleep as Charlemagne simply sat at his sleeping bag for another five minutes before doing the same.

Act 3, Scene 4

The next morning, approximately eight hours later, Diana and Tristan had awoken and had breakfast with Charlemagne. Charlemagne restarted the fire, which had burned out during the night, and they kept warm and ate for about an hour. Afterwards, they put their sleeping bags away and got ready to venture into the cave.

Charlemagne had equipped himself with various items, including two flashlights, and a blowtorch. Diana and Tristan each had their own flashlight, and Diana had her camera around her neck. They started their journey by travelling up the smooth steps behind them and climbing up to the narrow tunnel entering deeper into the cave. Charlemagne led them forward and they went on.

Tristan lowered his head with Diana as they went through the narrow tunnel entrance and came into a strange cavernous tunnel. The rock at their feet was smooth and stretched to the left at about a ninety degree angle. Likewise, the ceiling above them was at this same angle and there was only about a five feet gap between the floor and the ceiling, which required them to keep their heads low. On their right, at the end of the slope, were jagged rocks facing out. The rocks were sharp. The tunnel continued onward for about fifty meters.

The color of the rocks in the cave were a light grey and there was no other sound than their footsteps on the smooth rock, which echoed around them. The trio came to the end of the entrance tunnel and arrived at a smaller tunnel that was about four feet tall and led into a small chamber.

Charlemagne and the kids entered the chamber. The floor was immediately different from the smooth stone floor behind them, but instead composed of various loose stones and rocks at their feet. In addition, the ceiling was high, but converged at an extremely small, jagged tunnel that went upwards into the unknown. Charlemagne shined his light at the tunnel in the ceiling and then over to a circular tunnel going onwards into the cave. He led them out of the small chamber and deeper into the cavern.

The small chamber led into a seven foot tall chamber with smooth stone floors and walls. There were puddles in the floor, and the chamber extended for another fifty feet when it started to narrow and ceiling began to climb down, forcing them to duck their heads and crouch onwards through a hole that widened out again.

The smooth stone surface of the cave led downwards to a pit where there were again loose rocks and stones around. Charlemagne stopped atop of this slope and looked down to the rocks before shining his light over to a hole that led forward down into another tunnel. However, there was something strange about this tunnel entrance. It's design was neat and chiseled. Charlemagne gently brought himself down the slope and towards the rocks before going over to the tunnel entrance. He shined his light into the tunnel and could see that it was a long tunnel going on with a changing surface around the perimeter.

Instead of smooth rock, the surface all around transformed into a smooth ice. The tunnel was also tall, about double the height of Charlemagne on either side, which made it square-shaped. The trend of loose stones on the ground transformed into ice.

"Amazing," Charlemagne remarked, continuing to shine his light. "An ice cave."

"What does that mean?" Tristan asked as he crouched down to rest a little.

"I have no idea," Charlemagne responded, "but it appears that the cave continues on and on, so let's not waste time."

"Do you have any idea where the meteorite is?" Diana asked as they started to walk towards the tunnel.

"Not a clue," Charlemagne replied. "I was hoping it would have been on that stone beach, but it wasn't, which perplexes me further."

The three of them continued to walk down the tunnel and when they reached the icy surfaces, their lights shined on the ice and caused light to travel through and reflect out. The ice appeared light blue to them at spaces where the light shined and dark blue beyond. The atmosphere quickly changed, and this part of the cave was noticeably colder than the former.

"Is this a lava tube?" Charlemagne questioned himself. "No, the corners are too sharp to be a lava tube."

The group continued to walk and walk until Charlemagne paused and looked around. He shined his light on the walls and then the ceiling of the tunnel.

"The tunnel here is more pronounced and structured than the previous sections of the cave," Charlemagne said to the kids. "I wonder where this tunnel leads to."

Charlemagne then continued to lead them forward for about a kilometer when they came to a junction. A second tunnel continued left and right at a diagonal angle and at a similar height and width as the last tunnel. The tunnel they were currently in continued forward as well.

"Which way do we go?" Tristan asked.

Charlemagne hesitated to answer as he shined his light at all three different options. He then focused onwards in the tunnel they had already picked and turned to the kids.

"Forward, I suppose," Charlemagne simply said. "I did not expect this either."

Charlemagne continued to walk forward in the ice cave, stopping once more as he shined his light at the ground. He crouched down and looked at the ice, bringing a gloved hand over the frost before starting to scrape it off with a scraper. There was something inside the ice – something metallic. Charlemagne started to pick at it, but the ice was hard. He then took out his blowtorch and began to light a fire into the ice, melting it to reveal the metallic item underneath.

A rail-line was under the ice, extending in either direction. Charlemagne turned off the blowtorch and set it on the side. He then sat down and looked to the kids.

"We're in an abandoned mine," Charlemagne stated. "The meteorite is nowhere to be seen, and I have no idea what to do."

"What is this? An ice mine?" Diana asked, sitting down and turning off her flashlight.

"No," Charlemagne simply responded. "Although, that does make me wonder as to how all this ice got here in the first place."

"How does ice usually form like this?" Tristan then asked.

"Typically, this ice is perennial, meaning it comes and goes year round and forms because we are in a space that is below freezing," Charlemagne answered. "The second condition is that there must be a source of water that goes through the cave."

Charlemagne paused for a moment and then looked up at the ceiling with close eyes.

"I understand," Charlemagne said, looking back over to the kids. "The reason why I didn't find the meteorite immediately at the beach where we slept on is because of the changing seasons. We're currently in winter (or at least, it will be officially winter tomorrow) but that means ice forms and temperatures drop. Almost the entire surface of the Arctic Ocean is covered in perennial ice that forms in this time period until the spring when temperatures warm up, although not by a significant amount.

With almost the entire surface of the ocean covered by ice, the sea levels cannot adjust with tides as usual. However, in the spring and until the ice begins to form again, there is almost no ice, which allows the ocean to flex up and down with typical tides."

Charlemagne stood up and brought a hand to the ice.

"The ice isn't deep, which means it hasn't been like this for long," Charlemagne stated. "My guess is that it's been like this for less than a couple of months. With daily tides, water flows in up and down – that same water goes into the cave and comes out into this abandoned mine. A meteorite floating into the cave would eventually find its way through that same cave we just went through and eventually into this mine. In the winter, it would have settled somewhere around – most likely encased in ice because leftover moisture quickly freezes and creates these layers of ice over a small time frame until the tides stop altogether for the season."

"How come layers form on these rocks and not the rocks in the cavern?" Diana asked.

"I would have to guess that the rock of this mine is different than the rock of the cave we were just in," Charlemagne responded. "Possibly basalt or granite in the cave, and limestone here."

Charlemagne then shined his light down either side of the tunnels.

"My meteorite is somewhere down here, and I just need to figure out where it is to find it," Charlemagne said with heightened enthusiasm. "Come along, we need to find this rock of mine."

Charlemagne put his blowtorch away and continued forward along the cavern. The group passed about three different junctions until they started to reach the end of the tunnel. It was a dead-end. Charlemagne shined his light around the dead-end and then turned around. He led the kids back to the other side of the tunnel, reaching the first junction they came across. Charlemagne then took out something from his backpack. It was a hatchet.

With the hatchet, Charlemagne began to carve into the ice leading into the cavern, the words 'Exit' and into the tunnel leading to the dead-end they just came across, he carved '#1.' He then looked left and right and began to go left with the kids. They went down another mile long tunnel.

Charlemagne kept his flashlight pointed forward into the darkness. They eventually found the end and began to speed up. At the end of the tunnel, the path went down and around a circular chamber with a tall ceiling, all the way to the base of the chamber.

The surface of the walls in the chamber were strange. From the height of the tunnel below, the surface was composed of ice like the rest of the mineshaft, but above, it was made of a whiter ice – snow that blended with the ice. Charlemagne shined his flashlight around at the snow and then upwards to the ceiling where dozens of stalactites pointed downwards at them. Below, the ground was made of a dark ice.

Charlemagne shined his light at something directly ahead in the wall of ice and then towards the floor. He saw a reflection come back at him, which caused him to immediately travel down the path to the ice. He couldn't see what was in the thick ice because of the darkness and fact that the flashlight wouldn't penetrate any deeper inwards. Charlemagne instead took out his hatchet and began to swing at the ice but made a minor incision. He removed his backpack and started to rummage for the blowtorch.

The blowtorch threw a flame and Charlemagne began to burn through the ice towards the shiny piece of metal buried in the snow. He weakened the ice a bit and then set the blowtorch on the ground, still on. The kids were focused on the ground as Charlemagne took the hatchet and started to chop at the ice again. The metallic object was deep in the ice.

Tristan continued to watch, providing light with his flashlight alongside Diana. He then looked over to the blowtorch as it melted ice on the wall in front of them and ran water towards Charlemagne. Charlemagne took his blowtorch and shut it off. Tristan then brought his flashlight up at the wall as he noticed something near the corner between the floor and the wall – something buried within. He shined his light in and then jumped at the sight of what was behind it. Tristan's eyes looked in horror.

"Tristan, I need light," Charlemagne ordered.

"Look," Tristan instead replied.

Charlemagne looked up for a moment and then back down. He then paused and looked up slowly at what he was looking at. Diana followed and shined her light.

Inside the ice was a man, a large man, either a very large man with a single large white-fur lined red wool coat, or a thin man with various layers of coats underneath each other. His eyes were open slightly and arms crossed. He also wore a red tophue at the top of his head and had a thick white beard around his face. His eyes were light blue like Charlemagne's. At his feet were black boots.

Charlemagne's blowtorch had caused the ice around the foot to melt alongside a thin layer over the entire body. Charlemagne stood up and looked over to the man. He brought his hand over the ice to wipe some of the melted water down and get a clearer look.

"My God," Charlemagne remarked. "Help me free him."

Diana took a step back as Charlemagne lit the blowtorch and started to melt the rest of the ice from the foot up. It was a slow process, and within a couple of minutes, they had freed the legs and a good layer had melted off from the body due to radiating heat. Charlemagne stood up to wipe some sweat from his forehead. He then looked at the man. The man looked back at him. Charlemagne jumped

"Christ, he's alive!" Charlemagne shouted, reigniting the torch.

Charlemagne didn't have to reignite the torch as the rest of the ice had broken free and the man fell forward onto the ground.

"Help me lift him," Charlemagne asked Tristan.

"He's too heavy!" Tristan complained, trying to nudge him over.

"Damn, you're right!" Charlemagne shouted. "We'll have to pull him out of here and get him some immediate medical attention. I'm going to have to perform some first aid first."

Tristan and Charlemagne rolled the man onto his stomach. Charlemagne then brought his ear to the man's mouth to listen.

"Airway is clear," Charlemagne said, bringing his hands to the man's rib cage. "Equal expansion of the rib cage."

Charlemagne then brought a hand to the man's face.

"He's showing signs of shock, but he's got lots of layers on and should have gone into shock a long time ago. Let's pull him to the submarine and get him onboard. There's oxygen onboard and we'll have to get him to the Ingstad STAT."

"Aye," Tristan replied.

Act 4, Scene 1

Charlemagne returned to the cave alone and went forward through the cavern to get to the abandoned mine again. First, he searched around the encased ice for any clues as to how the man was entrapped but couldn't find anything left behind.

Once Charlemagne was finished, he proceeded to return to working on getting the shards of metal under the ice free with a blowtorch. The fire penetrated the ice and caused a puddle to form. Charlemagne then took an axe and hacked at the loose bits until he could scoop the shard out and look at it. It was light. It was hard. It was a piece of alien alloy about the size of a dinner plate. He set it on the ground, laid against the ice wall and then turned off his flashlight to listen to the emptiness and silence of the cave.

Charlemagne took deep breaths and sat in the cold for about ten minutes before picking up his flashlight, turning it on and then picking up the alien alloy. He put it in his backpack and then stood up to return to the submarine.

• •

Charlemagne looked into the patient room aboard the Ingstad as Dr. Vidkunsen examined the unconscious patient. From the mines, he had been brought to the sick bay where he was stripped of his layers and left in his old-fashioned trousers. He had a blood pressure cuff around his right upper arm and had various nodes across his bare hairy chest. He also had a clip at his right ring finger. His vitals displayed a low blood pressure and heart rate, but he was alive. Once the doctor was finished examining him, she exited the room, closing the door behind her and turning to face Charlemagne.

"I can't believe it, but he's going to be okay," Dr. Vidkunsen said to Charlemagne. "Tell me, is it true? You found him encased in ice?"

"Yes," Charlemagne responded. "You can ask the kids as well – Tristan was the one that found him. I just... I'm amazed that we were able to get him out and that he was able to survive who knows how long in there. I cannot suspect that it was long, but if my previous hypothesis about the ice in that cavern is true, it must've been in the minimum a couple of months."

"He could be the first case of cryogenics – no matter how long it was," Vidkunsen said. "He's showing no other abnormalities other than the hypothermia he evaded."

"Have you seen his clothing?" Charlemagne observed aloud.

The patient was not dressed in a pajamas and sitting in a hospital bed. All of his layers had been taken off so that the doctor could properly assess the patient.

"He had a large fur coat and a set of boots that looked like they weren't factory-made. His hat was almost exclusively Scandinavian, which matches his blue eyes and fair skin."

"Yes," Dr. Vidkunsen replied. "He must be from Greenland in that case. I'll continue monitoring him until he regains consciousness."

"Good," Charlemagne responded. "I'm going to go back into the mines – alone this time – to collect those pieces of metal I missed out on in the ice. It's strange – the cave I deduced the meteorite to have gone into led into an abandoned mine, but that also begs the question of what this man was doing in an abandoned mine."

"An explorer from one of the villages that must've gotten lost," Dr. Vidkunsen replied.

"How different would Norwegian be from Danish?" Charlemagne wondered.

"I could communicate with him if he spoke it," Dr. Vidkunsen replied. "Assuming he even speaks Danish."

Charlemagne nudged the doctor as he saw the patient beginning to wake up. The doctor immediately entered the room. Charlemagne walked over to stand by the doorway.

"*Hallo*," Dr. Vidkunsen greeted. "*Hvordan har du det?*"

"*Hvor er jeg?*" the man replied.

"*Du er ombord pa forskningsskipet Ingstad*," Dr. Vidkunsen replied. "*Hva heter du?*"

"*Ved du ikke, hvem jeg er? Jeg er kong Kristoffer den tiende af Hvitrnord!*" the man replied as though he was insulted by the question.

"What is he saying?" Charlemagne questioned the doctor.

"I asked him what his name was, and he questioned why I didn't know him. He claims he is King Kristoffer the Tenth of Hvitrnord," the doctor translated.

"Yes," the man replied in English.

The man spoke in a coarse Nordic accent.

"English – I speak English too," the man said.

"Good," Charlemagne responded, entering the room and going to the foot of the man's bed. "My name is Charlemagne de la Cabernet. What do you remember prior to waking up now?"

"I – I don't know," the man responded. "I don't remember anything."

"Right, well, my team and I found you in the depths of an abandoned mineshaft where you were encased in ice. We managed to thaw the ice and by some miracle, you were still alive. Tell me, what year is it?"

"What a stupid question," the man responded, looking around the room at the various advanced medical equipment. "It's... it's the year 1929 of course."

Charlemagne swallowed his breath and looked to the doctor. He smiled as he looked back at the man named Kristoffer.

"Funny," Charlemagne remarked. "What year do you remember it really being."

"Do you think I am funny?" the man questioned in insult, removing the nodes from his chest and shaking off the clip at his finger. "I have no time for this funny business – I have to return to my castle and get back to work."

"Sir, what castle?" Dr. Vidkunsen replied as the man got out of bed. "Please, you are not well enough to leave. We are on a boat."

"Then take me back to my home!" the man threatened. "I have to see my wife and my kids! I have only so much time before Christmas!"

"What happens on Christmas?" Charlemagne asked him.

"What happens on Christmas?" the man replied in a mocking tone. "Christmas is the most important date in the year for me – it is the time where the little children open their presents that I deliver to them. Do you really not know who I am?"

"I'm afraid not," Charlemagne responded. "Please, explain to me."

"I am Kristoffer, son of Kristoffer the Ninth, the great king of Hvitrnord and owner of the Kristoffersen Toys!" the man said to him. "Do you not know the brand?"

"No," Charlemagne said to him. "Sir, I'm afraid I have some bad news that might be shocking to you when you first hear it. You see, like I said earlier, I found you entrapped in ice and thought you were dead. If you truly believe you are in the year 1929, I'm afraid that is not true. In fact, it is currently the year 2018 – December 22nd, 2018."

"You lie," the man responded, taking a step back.

"It is true," Charlemagne said, taking a step forward. "I mean, look around you."

The man looked around himself.

"No…" the man said, shaking his head. "It – it cannot be true. My wife… my children…"

"Have lived, and most likely… lived on," Charlemagne said in a somber tone.

"I do not believe you!" the man yelled, slamming a fist on the end table next to him. "You, Mr. Cabernet, is it not?"

"Yes, Charlemagne Cabernet," Charlemagne stated.

"Cabernet – of the Cabernet clan?"

"That is right," Charlemagne nodded. "You seem to know who I am?"

"Not you, but Pepin Cabernet," the man responded. "He is the owner of the Cabernet Corporation. Is he not?"

"Pepin Cabernet was my great grandfather," Charlemagne responded. "He is dead now. I am his great grandson and owner of Cabernet Industries."

"Lies – all lies," the man shouted, pushing the end table over. "Why do you persist with this joke?"

"Mr. Kristoffersen," Charlemagne stated in a strict voice. "We are not joking around here. My colleague, Dr. Vidkunsen, has assessed you and I have found you. You are aboard a ship roaming the Arctic Ocean, and this town of yours called Hvitrnord and company, Kristoffersen Toys, no longer exists. I'm sorry, but you are in the future. No means of violence can bring the past back – I'm afraid you will just have to cope with this truth."

The man shook his head and tilted it over. He looked down on the ground in silence. Charlemagne looked to the doctor who had looked to him with worry. She then went to Charlemagne and guided him out with her. They closed the door behind them.

"Perhaps we should leave Mr. Kristoffersen alone for the time being," Dr. Vidkunsen reasoned. "To learn that it is the year 2018 from being from the year 1929 (if that is true) is a shocking moment. If it is not true, then whatever is wrong with this man should be seen by the appropriate specialist. I'm worried of the implications of bringing this man aboard."

"Aye, doctor," Charlemagne responded as they walked down the corridor and away from the bedroom. "However, what else can we do with the man? We're in the middle of the arctic with no trace of modern civilization for miles. We will have to cope with him as he will have to cope with the truth."

Tristan entered the infirmary wing upon hearing Charlemagne's last sentence. He was with Diana and walked over to them.

"What's up?" Tristan asked.

"Our friend has awoken," Charlemagne explained. "I also found this in the mine," he added, opening his backpack to take out the tablet of alien alloy he had found. "Here."

Tristan took the piece of alien alloy in his hand and looked at it. He then passed it to Diana.

"Neat," Tristan remarked. "So, what's the deal with him?"

"Well…" Charlemagne said."

Charlemagne told the kids a brief synopsis of the conversation that had just occurred.

"Oh my God…" Diana said under her breath before hitting Tristan in the shoulder. "He's Santa Claus."

"What?" Tristan questioned. "Weren't you listening? His name is Kristoffer – not Klaus, and by the way he's been treating Dr. Vidkunsen, he doesn't sound like a saint."

"Who cares? He's a big old man with a white beard who owns a factory that makes toys – that's Santa Claus. We have to visit this Hvitrnord – I bet it's his little village!" Diana remarked.

"Diana, please," Charlemagne responded, holding tablet of alien alloy at his side. "We do not even know if this man is sane."

"We don't even know if Diana is sane," Tristan muttered.

Diana hit Tristan in the shoulder again.

"Mr. Cabernet," a frail voice said from behind them.

The group turned to see Kristoffer on his feet under the doorway. Dr. Vidkunsen immediately stepped forward.

"My friend, please return to bed – you are not well enough to be on your feet."

"I am fine," Kristoffer insisted, "but Mr. Cabernet, please, I do not believe that it has been ninety years."

"I'm sorry, but if you say that you last remember it being the year 1929, then I'm afraid that it is true. We are in the future," Charlemagne said, crossing his arms.

"What is that?" Kristoffer questioned, pointing at the meteorite in Diana's hands. "I recognize that texture and form."

Kristoffer stepped forward and walked over to the group. The doctor took a step back as he got closer. The man walked like a zombie towards them. He then motioned his fingers for Diana to give him the meteorite.

"If you'd please," Kristoffer asked.

Diana handed the meteorite to him.

"Yes," Kristoffer said, holding the meteorite. "*Mjolnium*."

"Mjolnium?" Charlemagne questioned, turning to the doctor. "What does that mean?"

"Uh…" the doctor replied, hesitating for a moment. "I'm not sure. It's just gibberish."

"This is mjolnium – it is what we called this material," Kristoffer explained. "From the skies… we collected great amounts of this material and used it to create certain toys for the children. It was a good material – difficult to melt, but it is possible with the right materials and patience."

Kristoffer handed the rock back to Diana.

"You had more of this material?" Charlemagne questioned.

"At my castle, yes," Kristoffer responded, looking to Charlemagne with plain eyes.

"Your castle in this town of Hvitrnord?" Charlemagne then asked.

"Yes," Kristoffer responded. "Take me to my village, and I will show you the reserves of this alloy in my castle."

Charlemagne looked at the man with hesitant eyes. He nodded to him.

"I'll see what I can do," Charlemagne simply said, clearing his throat. "How about you go back to bed? I'll speak with the captain, and we'll look into the status of your village."

• •

Charlemagne searched for Allodia and found her in a room behind the cargo hold. It was a small room with a table in the middle and various shelves against the wall. She had her laptop next to a map of the Arctic Circle. There were pins over certain locations on the various islands. He approached her as she looked up and over to him.

"What's up?" Allodia asked.

"I have a favor to ask," Charlemagne said, walking up to the opposite side of the table.

"What is it now?" Allodia responded.

"Our cryogenic friend has awoken and says that he comes from a small village in Greenland known as Hvitrnord. Does this village name mean anything to you? Is it on your list of villages to visit?"

"Hvitrnord?" Allodia repeated before looking down.

Next to her laptop was a set of papers stapled in the corner together. Allodia began to go through the various village names on the list, tracing her finger down before stopping.

"Yes," Allodia confirmed before looking on the map. "Here."

Charlemagne looked at the location of the village. It was close to where the abandoned mine was. However, it was nowhere near where they were now – in the Baffin Bay.

"We made a stop at the village when you were out," Allodia reported. "It was a nice and small village."

"I need to go back to it – so that we can drop off this man," Charlemagne explained. "Is there any way of doing that?"

"I'm sorry, Charlie, but we can't go back. We're on a set path from here on out. Some of our most important visits are in the next couple of days too."

"Fine, then let me take the helicopter and fly out to the village. Please," Charlemagne requested. "Otherwise, this poor man won't be able to return home."

Allodia frowned at her brother.

"We need that helicopter to make drops at these villages. How else are we going to stop at over a hundred different settlements in the course of the next couple of days?" Allodia questioned. "Not to mention fuel – we already dipped into our emergency fuel supplies getting your friend to this boat and then you back to the submarine."

Charlemagne didn't reply. Allodia sighed.

"There's no point in arguing," Allodia muttered. "Fine, I'll talk to Gerald about flying you over to Hvitrnord, but he is coming right back. Understood? You also get one trip back because we can't afford to waste any more fuel."

"I won't ask anymore from you – I promise," Charlemagne responded with a light smile. "Thank you, Allodia."

Act 4, Scene 2

The next day, Charlemagne, Kristoffer, Diana, and Tristan exited the Ingstad and came to the helipad at the stern of the boat where Gerald Bell, a member of the Cabernet Foundation who travelled with Allodia and happened to be a licensed helicopter pilot, was in the cockpit of the cargo helicopter. The rotors were spinning and the helicopter was ready for take-off.

"What is this machine?" Kristoffer asked, hesitant to step closer to the helicopter.

"We call them 'helicopters' and they're like aeroplanes, except that they're for shorter distances and hover instead of fly," Charlemagne explained. "Come along now, we haven't got much time and are on a tight schedule. This machine will take you home."

Charlemagne waved for Kristoffer to come over to the helicopter. He then helped him into the craft. Kristoffer was dressed in his old fur coat and boots. He also wore his hat. The kids got into the helicopter and sat in one of the seats available to them behind the cockpit. Charlemagne helped Kristoffer fasten his seatbelt and then gave the all clear to the helicopter pilot so that they could take-off.

Bell wore a pilot helmet and shades over his eyes. He also had a standard orange parka jacket and ski trousers that everybody else wore, but in differing styles and colors. The helicopter lifted up and then began to make its way away from the ship before going north towards Hvitrnord.

In less than an hour, the helicopter travelled nearly two-hundred kilometers to reach the coast where a small village waited for them. The helicopter made a gentle descent downwards onto a clearing. Bell then gave them the thumbs up to exit. Charlemagne detached his seatbelt and then went forward to the cockpit.

"Do you mind waiting a moment or two," Charlemagne requested. "I'm not sure how long I'll be staying and would rather update you sooner rather than later."

"You've got ten minutes, Mr. Cabernet, and then I have to get back to Ms. Cabernet with this helicopter or she'll have my tail."

"Thank you," Charlemagne responded, stepping back and going over to open the hatch for them to exit. "Welcome to Hvitrnord, my friend."

Kristoffer struggled to detach his seatbelt, but once he did, he stood up and then hopped down to the ground to look out to the small village. Kristoffer held a frown as he looked at the hamlet. Diana and Tristan stood together as they looked at what they all saw.

Ahead of them was a group of single-story houses with flat roofs spread across an area of land next to the coast. Near the coast were a series of steel storage tanks behind chain-link fences. The housing structures were very uniform outside of their coloring, which varied between house to house. Other than the color, they were all the same size with cables and wires hanging from portable to portable. Other than these structures, the only other structures that stood out was an obvious church with a bell tower in the middle atop the entrance and some greenhouses.

The skies were cloudy and dark due to the permanent polar night and lights shined across the town and some coming from within the houses. There were no roads and snow covered the enter ground, but not in a dramatic amount as none of the houses were covered or blocked in a deep layer. At most, the snow appeared to have reached about a foot high based on some layers over the rooftops.

"No," Kristoffer said, looking around, "this is not Hvitrnord. I do not know what this village is, but that it is the most disenchanting settlement I have ever seen. There is no beauty in this village. How can there even be life here?"

Charlemagne looked at the large man with a worried look.

"It has been eighty-nine years," Charlemagne stated, reminding him. "You should have perhaps expected it to have changed in those eighty-nine years."

"No," Kristoffer repeated, "change had nothing to do with this – this is not Hvitrnord. The coastline, the houses – it is all different."

"Right," Charlemagne responded. "How about we go into town and speak to some of the villagers. Perhaps someone can help us out."

Kristoffer and Charlemagne began walking over to the village. Diana and Tristan walked behind them and followed as they went towards the houses. Without having to go to any of the homes, curious residents exited outside over the noise of the helicopter and looked over to Charlemagne and Kristoffer.

"*Hallo?*" a man called out to them.

"Hello!" Charlemagne shouted back. "Could you help us?"

"*En Engelskmand…*" someone from around muttered.

"*Hvad er det her for et sted?!*" Kristoffer questioned in a loud and booming voice. "*Dette er ikke Hvitrnord!*"

The residents of the town began to murmur to each other. None of them spoke to the foreigners and simply just looked at them.

"*Jeg er kong Kristoffer den tiende, og jeg kraever at vide, hvad der er sket med mit rige!*"

The people continued to murmur to each other, but in a more annoyed manner with slight worry as they looked at Kristoffer as if he were some sort of lunatic. Charlemagne looked at the residents and then to Kristoffer. He then looked over to the people.

"Does anybody here speak English?!" Charlemagne shouted. "We need help!"

Tristan looked on as nobody responded. He frowned.

"Please, does anybody here speak English? German? French?" Charlemagne shouted in desperation. "Anybody?"

Tristan eyes shot over to the sound of a door shutting. A man had exited his home and looked over to Charlemagne. Most of the residents had white skin and fair colored hair either blonde, light brown (dark blonde), or reddish-colored hair. The man who had shut his door had a blonde beard and wore a knit cap over his head. He looked to be in his late thirties or perhaps forties and waved to Charlemagne.

"*Yoohoo*," the man said. "I speak English," he then added in a thick Danish accent.

"Oh, good," Charlemagne whispered to himself. "Hello, my good sir. My name is Charlemagne Cabernet and we need help."

"Hello," the man said, walking over to him.

The two of them met. Charlemagne offered his hand for a handshake, but the man simply looked at his hand and refused to remove his own from within his coat.

"My name is Lars Jensen," the man replied. "What can we do for you?"

"What is this place?" Kristoffer immediately said to him with fury in his voice. "Why do you call this place Hvitrnord?"

"Please," Charlemagne replied to Kristoffer. "Let me speak to him."

Charlemagne then turned to Lars.

"Sorry, but I'm a scientist that was doing research at an old abandoned mine not too far from here when we found this man entrapped in the ice. He states that he is from the year 1929 and the former king of a local village close to here known as Hvitrnord. I know, it might sound farfetched, but it is the truth. I've brought him here and he does not believe this to be the right place. Could you possibly shed some light – rather, do you know this man? Or better yet, do you know the history of this town?"

"Oh," Lars replied. "I better take you to my great-grandmother. She is an elder of this town and has lived almost a hundred years. Come, she might be able to help you if what you are saying is true."

"Perfect," Charlemagne responded with little glee in his voice. "Come along then, Kristoffer. This man is going to help us."

Kristoffer marched with Charlemagne northwards. Diana and Tristan lagged behind as witnesses. Lars brought them to one of the huts northmost of the village. They stopped outside and went up the steps to the top of a small porch where the front entrance was. Lars then knocked on the door and then opened the door.

"*Bedstemor, jeg har besogende her til dig,*" Lars said, closing the door behind him.

Charlemagne could hear a frail voice inside. The door opened again and Lars ushered them inside. The inside of the portable home was warm. The floorboards sounded hollow and had a thin carpet overtop. The composition of the house was like a recreational vehicle with a kitchen at one-side, a table on the opposite side, a living room at the far-end, and a narrow corridor going towards a bedroom and bathroom in the other end. The decoration of the house was a little more traditional and homelier. Charlemagne walked over to where there was a skinny and small old lady in an armchair with a TV in front of her. She had a blanket over her lap and wore a red sweater. In front of her and the TV was a small couch.

"This is my great-grandmother, Anne Jansen," Lars said, introducing her to the group as they found a place to sit in the living room.

Lars began to move some chairs from the dining table over to the kitchen so that he and the kids could sit down.

"*Hallo,*" the woman said in a weak voice. "*Hvem er du?*"

"*Dette er Charlemagne og Kristoffer. Jeg er ikke sikker pa, hvem de to born er.*"

"*Sid ned,*" the old woman insisted with a jovial smile.

"*Kong Kristoffer,*" Kristoffer corrected to the man as he sat down on the couch with Charlemagne. "*Je ger kongen af Hvitrnord og son af Kristoffer den niende.*"

The woman looked over to Kristoffer.

"*Du ligner bestemt den gamle konge…*" the old woman said.

"Could you translate for me please?" Charlemagne requested to Lars as Kristoffer continued to speak in Danish to the old woman.

"She said that he looks like the old king," Lars repeated for Charlemagne. "He then said that it good to finally meet someone who knows what is going on. He is now asking her what has happened to Hvitrnord."

The old woman, Anne, proceeded to look up and then over to Kristoffer as she spoke.

"She is saying that the town had moved in the forties and that they had to abandon the old village after the king had disappeared."

"*Je ger kongen! Jeg forsvandt ikke – jeg var fanget i is!*" Kristoffer replied in a loud voice, but not in a hostile manner.

"He says that he was not gone, but that he was trapped in ice," Lars translated.

"Yes," Charlemagne nodded, turning over to the woman as she began to speak again.

"My *oldemor* is saying that after the king had vanished, the toy industry quickly came to an end, which brought the town into bad times. They attempted to survive by selling raw resources, but nobody would buy them. She is now saying that the town tried to do as he as king had asked – to open the town to trade and the global market, but that it ultimately did not do them good because resources were limited."

"*Hvorfor flytte byen?*" Kristoffer questioned the old woman.

"Your friend just asked, 'Why move the town?'" Lars translated as the old woman continued explaining. "She is saying that about ten years after your friend had disappeared, the town was visited by the Germans who took interest in some of our resources but were kicked out by the Americans a couple of years later. The Americans occupied the town and brought lots of military men with them, but they didn't like the location of the town since the old inlet would freeze over in the winter and was shallow. They also discovered sources of oil and natural gas nearby, so they moved the town closer to a port where the water was deep and ice wouldn't melt and built these homes for the residents to live in and work for them. The old town was abandoned in favor of this town, which was seen as more modern with natural gas heating and jobs. However, the Americans didn't stay and eventually we ran out of gas and oil, so all our good luck came to an end."

"*Og sa?*" Kristoffer asked.

The woman paused for a moment. She then continued to speak.

"Thanks to the Americans, a lot of residents from the old village left and went to study in the United States. Very few returned because of the poor economic situation. We tried to survive by exporting traditional goods that we hunted and caught, but in the eighties, a lot of these items were said to be bad and rejected from the public market. By the nineties, we had become a poorer town and dependent on welfare from the Danish government."

"*Min Gud,*" Kristoffer reacted, "*og hvad skete der med min kone og born?*"

"Your friend just asked, 'What happened to my wife and kids?'"

The old woman paused and thought for a moment. She then looked to Kristoffer with an apologetic face.

"*Undskyld, men jeg ved det ikke. Jeg var bare en lille pige dengang...*"

Kristoffer frowned and then stood up. He walked behind the couch and stroked his beard. He looked saddened.

"*Hvorfor forlod du os?*" the old woman asked.

"*Jeg forlod dig ikke, kvinde. Jeg kan ikke huske, hvordan jeg endte dernede,*" Kristoffer replied to her.

"What are they saying?"

"She asked me, 'Why did I leave [them]?'" Kristoffer translated to Charlemagne. "I told her that I did not leave them, but that I still do not remember what happened before I was trapped in that ice. I do not wish to remember – I worry about my wife and children. I want to know what happened to them."

Charlemagne took a deep breath as he lay back in the couch.

"I have no idea of how to help you with that," Charlemagne remarked. "If the elder of this village doesn't know what happened, then I'm not sure who could find out."

"Take me to the old village," Kristoffer demanded.

"I…"

"If you want your precious materials, you will have to take me to that village," Kristoffer reminded him.

"Yes," Charlemagne responded. "I know that, but I don't have the slightest of an idea of how to do that."

Kristoffer then looked over to the woman.

"*Bare rolig, gamle kvinde, for din konge er vendt tilbage,*" Kristoffer said to her before turning to Lars. "*Fortael emnerne, at deres konge er vendt tilbage. Vi vender tilvage til den gamle landsby og abner min fabrik gen.*"

"What are you telling them?" Charlemagne questioned.

"I am telling them that their king has returned and that I will take care of them," Kristoffer summarized. "We are going to visit the old village."

Act 4, Scene 3

The next morning, after being allowed to lodge in the village of Hvitrnord, the group found themselves in twilight in the late morning by some sleds and some villagers. Thanks to the help of Lars, he managed to put together a small expedition group from some of the men in the village and borrow some dogs so that they could go visit the old village. The dogs had white fur that blended in with the surrounding snowy ground.

There were three sleds in total for the eight of them, three people for the first two and then two on the last as Kristoffer was a large man. There were about thirty dogs in total, ten for each sled. Diana was busy getting to know each dog as she made her way petting each of them with Tristan as they waited on some last minute preparations. The dogs were Greenlander Dogs, or *Grønlandshunden*, which was a large dog with thick fur. They came in varying light colors and had tails that rolled up. They had pointed, triangle ears and large heads. Each of the dogs appeared to be fit and muscular compared to the average dog.

Charlemagne took the long-range satellite radio he had and placed it on his belt. The helicopter left while Charlemagne and Kristoffer were talking to Lars' great-grandmother yesterday. He then took both hands to the map in his other hand and looked at the northern coast of Greenland on the map. Charlemagne had made a mark on the map between their location and the location of the underwater cave and abandoned mine shafts at least five kilometers from the village at a neighboring fjord.

"Mr. Charlemagne," Lars said to him. "We're ready to leave."

"Very good," Charlemagne responded, looking over to Kristoffer.

"Good," Kristoffer said, going over to a sled. "Let us go at once!"

Kristoffer hopped aboard one of the sleds and took the reins of the dogs. Charlemagne then boarded behind him, sitting on the back bench with the map in his hand. Lars took a sled where the kids were loading themselves atop. Tristan sat at the back with his legs open so that Diana could sit in front of him. The third sled was occupied by the three additional villagers who would go with them.

Kristoffer whipped the reins and sent the dogs rushing forward. The rope attached to the dogs converged at a central knot from the sled and then spread out so that the dogs ran in a fan-shape. Kristoffer led the group out with the two other sleds following from behind. They took off from the village and began to make their way towards the flat rolling plains of snow in the distance.

The sled began to make their approach towards a canyon between the hills. Once through the canyon, they came to a large clearing of snow that stretched out left and right for a couple miles before reaching cliffs of rock that went up to plateaus of snow. Diana and Tristan looked out around them at the vastness of snow.

"This is nothing like Russia," Diana remarked, looking out. "It's also still nothing like I expected the Arctic to be."

"Yeah, I have to agree with you on that one," Tristan replied.

Charlemagne looked at the map and then out and around the plains from where they left the village. He kept doing this to make sure they were on the right path as they ventured into inner depths of Greenland to cut through to the old village.

The sleds only went as fast as the dogs could run with all the weight behind them. All that the kids could do was lie back and enjoy the scenery in the limited light around them, which wasn't much at this time of the day, especially due to the clouds.

Ahead of them in the horizon was a wall of steep rock covered in further ice and snow. The sleds aimed for a canyon between the rocks. The sleds converged at the canyon opening and began to make another pass through some narrow rocks before coming out to another clearing of snow. On the right, instead of there being a cliff of rocks in the distance, there was instead a hill of snow going upwards. In the northwest, there was low mountain covered entirely in snow in the distance. To the left, there was a good mile or two of plain snow followed by cliffs of snow and ice. The sled made their way towards the side of the mountain, approaching the side and making a pass to towards the further plains in the distance.

The plains past the low mountain brought them to a simple space where the horizons rolled up to some simple hills. The sleds then went downhill and approached a lower clearing where they made their way towards a steep edge of rock decorated in sprinkles of snow. From there, once they made it to the rocks, they began to turn left and follow the side of the rock westward. The height of the rocks from where they started was roughly fifty feet, but as they continued for several minutes to the side, the height shortened and blended into the landscape for them to climb up the coastline.

Charlemagne looked at the map and held his finger at the mouth of a fjord. He then looked to the side and outwards towards the frozen Arctic Ocean where the frozen ice stretched even further. The distance grew as they went higher atop of the coast and could see further, but that didn't change the landscape and instead stretched the ever long ice out. Diana looked out to the ocean and could see nothing abnormal in the distance. It was simply a sea of ice.

"There it is in the horizon," Kristoffer remarked, looking ahead. "Oh, my heart woes – what has happened to my poor kingdom?"

Charlemagne looked up from his map and forward, expecting to see a village on the coast, but instead, in the distance (perhaps another mile or two away) was the sideline of a smooth mountain and a hill in front of it. Atop of the hill was a castle, and below it was an entire village buried beneath snow with roofs poking out. Around the edge of the village was a stone wall, which demonstrated the boundaries of the village. The village itself appeared to be built atop of a plateau. The walls extended above the icy cliffs and went either side before wrapping around the base of the mountain to the left. The village was buried in snow as if there had been an avalanche from the neighboring mountain.

"From what I can see," Charlemagne responded, "neglect and abandonment."

"Damn the Americans for forsaking my people!" Kristoffer shouted.

Tristan tightened his grip around Diana as he looked at the village to get her attention.

"I bet you didn't expect that," Tristan said to her.

"Nope," Diana responded.

The sleds again began to go downwards atop of the coastline, rolling down and then up, down and then up as they approached the town atop of a plateau. Behind Hvitrnord were tall mountains along the coast. Next to the town was the open sea with broken pieces of ice sitting atop of the surface. Charlemagne looked at the map and could see that the village was built on the other side of the fjord from where they were approaching, which led Charlemagne to suspect that the original mine was somewhere along the smooth mountain to the right. The sleds began to make an approach to the frozen fjord.

Charlemagne put his map away and simply looked over to where he saw a stone bridge constructed between the two sides of the fjord from where they were and over to the gates built into the wall that surrounded the former kingdom. The sleds diverted from the coast of the fjord and began to make their way over to the bridge, which was covered in snow. Snow poured out from the portcullis and it appeared that infiltrating through the walls seemed impossible.

Kristoffer brought the party to the mouth of the bridge. They got off from the sleds and took a break. Charlemagne walked over to the bridge and looked around while Kristoffer went straight forward to the gate of the wall.

"Right, we're here Kristoffer," Charlemagne said, walking over to him. "What now? There's no foreseeable manner in which we can enter – the town is buried in snow."

"We will have to go around to enter through the left side," Kristoffer remarked, walking away from the portcullis and back across the bridge. "My castle contains a treasure trove of material in its depths. You will find all the mjolnium you desire there. Come."

Charlemagne walked back over to the sled dogs where they were taking a break. He began to speak in Danish to Lars, pointing down the fjord and around to the side of the castle. Kristoffer than wagged a finger at him and turned to Charlemagne.

"Mr. Jensen insists on a break," Kristoffer remarked with displeasure. "Come, Charlemagne, we will continue on foot and walk to the castle."

Kristoffer picked up a rucksack from the sled and brought it around his shoulder. He then proceeded to walk over and down the coastline alone. Charlemagne looked at the kids and began to follow. Diana hit Tristan in the side as they were with the dogs and began to follow.

The fjord was not long, but it did take time for them to walk down and then around. Once at the base of the hill, they looked upwards and over to the distance they had to climb up on foot. Kristoffer did not hesitate and kept marching upwards.

"You know, this is a lot like being in the Egyptian desert, but instead of sand, there's nothing but snow, and instead of it being deathly hot, it's deathly cold..." Tristan said.

"I don't know which I'd prefer," Diana added.

Charlemagne lagged behind Kristoffer as he marched over the castle walls and then went looked up and over the houses. The snow was approximately two meters tall in depth. The town was buried, but the castle in the distance was not and stood atop the hill it was on. They made their way over to the castle, which was strangely constructed with a factory on the right-side. The factory was noticeable by the smokestacks that poked up from the roof.

The castle had a bailey, which led them into the courtyard. There was only a foot of snow at this height and the great big doors of the castle were directly across. The main entrance of the castle had two large round towers at either side. The towers went upwards and then converted into cone roofs approximately five-stories high. Kristoffer walked up to the tall wooden doors and pressed forward on them, opening them up. He then looked inside as a gust of cold air rushed in to the corridor leading out into another courtyard in the center of the castle.

"For over thirty generations, my family has lived in this castle and ruled this town," Kristoffer stated. "Since we came to Greenland almost nine-hundred years ago... or rather, almost a thousand years ago now."

Kristoffer walked into the castle and to the opposite side where they entered a large courtyard. A door on the left-side with a large glass window above it led into a church that was conjoined to the entire structure. Next to the church was a staircase that then went right and into the rear of the castle. On the other side of the church was a doorway going into one of the two circular towers. On the right was a large doorway going into the factory.

"Every Sunday, my people would come to the castle and we would gather in the church for Mass," Kristoffer remarked. "My wife loved Sunday for this reason."

"Right," Charlemagne replied. "What about the mjolnium?"

"My wife…" Kristoffer muttered. "What has become of her? What has become of my children?"

Kristoffer marched off and towards one of the larger doors. He pushed through and entered the castle interior. Charlemagne looked to the kids and then went after him. Tristan and Diana followed from behind. They followed him through a large room and came to a circular staircase going upwards. He then exited out and went down a long corridor that led to another staircase going upwards. From there, they came to a chamber – a bedroom. Kristoffer stopped at the foot of a bed where he was on his knees.

The bedroom was empty but was beautifully decorated. The bed sat across from a fireplace, which had a bathroom behind it. They were in the tallest room of one of the circular towers and could look out the glass windows to the rest of the town and beyond.

"She is not here," Kristoffer confessed. "I don't know where she could have gone."

Kristoffer then stood up and turned to the others.

"Just like on that night... I... I'm remembering now..." Kristoffer said, sitting on his bed. "I remember what happened because it was just like this.... My wife was missing..."

"What do you remember?" Charlemagne asked. "Focus..."

Diana and Tristan stood at the doorway. Each of them looked bored.

"Let me tell you what I remember," Kristoffer stated. "I was in this bedroom... and I could not find my wife."

Act 4, Scene 4

One thousand years ago, my ancestors came to Greenland on longships in search of a new home. We were outcasts in the old world and came looking for opportunity. In these times, the warm waters brought us to these unpopulated lands where we found hope for a new beginning. My great ancestor, King Kristoffer, the first king of Hvitrnord, found his pass-time in carpentry and in these lands they found an abundance of timber. With these resources, he crafted toys to bring smiles to the children and they found great joy in these toys. Our first king, enthralled by the joy he had brought to these children decided to go to the neighboring villages to do the same, and that became a tradition.

Kristoffer looked around his bedroom. A fire was lit at the fireplace and it was warm. A table in the corner played local tunes on a record player. Kristoffer was not dressed in a coat, but instead in a simple white wool tunic that went down just to the top of his knees. He also wore a pair of simple red linen hand-crafted trousers. At his feet, he had a pair of black hand-crafted boots made of leather with straps that went over the top portion around his ankles. Kristoffer stood up from the bed and went over to the window. From the window, he looked down at his town.

In the past, my people did not live in poorly constructed huts like those in New Hvitnord, but instead they lived in homes they could call homes. The homes were made of brick and had slanted roofs. The streets were made of cobblestone and were cleared day and night so that the carriages pulled by reindeer could pass the streets. There's nothing like that in the new village.

Kristoffer looked out to the village on the winter night. It was dark outside, but the town shined with light pouring from the homes of the villagers. Street lamps also lit the streets in a warm glow. People could be seen walking on the sides of the street, dressed in fur coats to keep them warm against the harsh arctic climate. The walls stretched along the entirety of the village and looked down the fjord and out to the arctic ocean, which was much like it was in the present – open water with chunks of ice floating around. There was a trail of broken ice from the port on the side of the town where ironclad ships sat with smoke pouring outwards from its stack like the many chimneys around.

Some of the houses of the village were split between shops on the ground floor and homes above. The shops had signs advertising each unique business from bookstores, to a toy store, to a dentist office to a general store. In the center of the town was a square plaza with a tall Christmas tree in the middle. Around the tree were various stalls where fishermen sold fish big and large as well as kelp harvested from the local sea. *A diet of walrus and helping of kelp was all that one needed to eat to survive back then. There were no microwaveable meals as we ate last night. There was no pasta or chicken – none of that nonsense! There was only what God had given to us to feed upon in these lands and that was all that we needed!*

Kristoffer turned around from the window and went towards a wardrobe. He opened the cabinet and took out a large white fur-lined dark red wool coat and placed it over his body. He also took out a red touphe that was lined with white fur as well. He put the hat over his head and the closed the wardrobe door. He then went to the door of his bedroom and left. He went down the stairs of the tower and could hear the echoes of chatter throughout his home. He came to a corridor and began to walk down. The corridor was lit by lamps with candles that hung from the walls.

In our homes, there was none of this electricity that you have now. We didn't need it as long as we could harvest enough fat and there was a lot of that to go around in the animals harvested in the town. We only needed fire as long as we had this source of fat to make soaps, candles, and other goods. There was coal in our town – a coal mine even. With our reliance on fire, we could pour our resources into different projects. We knew how to survive and didn't rely on the Danes to send us anything. For one-thousand years we never even knew of the existence of oil or these natural gases! Even at the top of the world, we didn't need any help to stay warm!

Kristoffer walked down a corridor and came to the courtyard of his home. He looked to the side and saw a servant dressed in white breeches and in a blue coat. He wore a similar touphe hat, but in the color blue. His boots were black and from his ankles to just under his knees, covering the breeches, he had long thick wool socks. He had fair skin that glowed in the snow around him and light blue eyes. He was young, baby-faced and had long light blonde hair that peaked out from underneath his hat. He was slightly shorter than the king by almost half a foot. He was young and pre-adolescent.

"My king," the man greeted, kneeling down on one knee.

"Rise, my son," Kristoffer stated, signaling for him to stand. "Where is your mother? I have not seen her all day and it is now dark out."

"I am sorry, father, but I do not know where mother is. Perhaps you should speak with Lord Monrad. I saw him in the factory last."

"Thank you," Kristoffer replied, patting his son on the shoulder.

My son, Kristoff, should have been my successor to the throne. Instead, he inherited nothing. He was young at this time, almost thirteen-years old and passionate with the same craft of his father. I only hope now that he lost a father and not parents.

Kristoffer passed his son and went diagonal across the courtyard to the steps that went up and then right into the rear of the castle. He went down a corridor to the end, opened a set of doors, and then went further along the current corridor before turning right to another set of double doors. He opened the doors and stepped forward to the balcony of the grand factory where below various workers were busy making toys as well as the material and pieces in the toys.

The atmosphere in the factory was warm. The workers were dressed in simple tunics that were dirty from all their intensive toymaking. Like Kristoffer's son, they also wore breeches, but instead of socks they had leg wraps from below their knees to their ankles with second-hand shoes at their feet. The average peasant was shorter than the king and his son by anywhere between a foot to half a foot. The factory floor was lively and a crowded space with many machines in the middle and front of the space and a simpler assembly line towards the end where toys were put together and then brought together to be shipped out. The factory was also a modern area with a functioning frame above the ceiling with a crane that moved about. Light fixtures hung from the ceiling and shined lights down as well. At the various workstations, workers punched holes into sheets of metal or pressed metal with metal to create unique pieces that would be part of certain towers. There were also stations with buzz saws slicing wooden planks and other machines spinning cotton.

The steam engine furnaces roared, and coal was thrown into the mouths of these hungry machines by workers underneath the platforms of the engines.

My factory ran like a clock with almost half the town employed and a part of the toy making. From the roots of this factory, it was just us sons of Kristoffer making and carving the toys out of wood, but now it was town-wide affair. Th entire factor ran under the supervision of a small group of my most trusted colleagues – my lords. On this date, it was Lord Monrad who was supervising the production in the factory.

Lord Monrad was dressed in grey trousers and a tailcoat as he supervised the factory workers. He looked at a pocket watch and then began to shout at a group of men who were smelting metals.

My grandfather revolutionized our town when he visited England and brought with him the secrets of steam mechanics. He created this factory, and through myself and my father, we modernized it to create a place where we could make toys at a faster pace than ever. You see, my family has always made toys as a pastime and then brought these toys to the children of the town and neighboring towns. It was what we did, but as time progressed, we began to sell these towns rather than give them because the more work we had to put in, the more expensive it became to produce each toy despite the ever-growing demand. Basic economics! Our toys were revered by not only our people, but our neighbors! A lot of the townsfolk were employed by us and we paid them for their work, which they would then put in to feed their families and sometimes buy these same toys from the local toyshop. Regardless, as a tradition, each year on Christmas Day, my company would ship toys to the various children of neighboring villages and bring smiles to the Nordic children of Greenland – great smiles!

Kristoffer walked down and over to Lord Monrad.

"My king," Monrad said. "How can I help you? Have you looked at the provisions of our new constitution? I hope that you sign it into law before the end of the year. We can start the year of 1930 on a grand note."

"Not now, Monrad, I am not here to argue over this constitution of yours. I am looking for my wife, Ole," Kristoffer stated. "Do you know where she is?"

"Klara? I'm afraid I haven't seen her since this morning," Lord Monrad answered, slightly annoyed. "Why?"

"I have not seen her all day and surely the miners have all returned home by now. I worry about her" Kristoffer asked. "It is unlike her to be out for this long, especially this late in September."

"It is possible," Kirk replied, shrugging. "If she hasn't returned, then it could mean that she is in trouble. Sire, in regard to this document, it is for the best of this town that we organize an elected council to oversee the mundane administration of everyday affairs. Look at yourself, in your age, you haven't even the time to look after your son and wife."

"I will not have my powers cut short," Kristoffer argued. "For almost a thousand years my family has reigned over these lands and it will not come to an end."

"Your reign will *not* come to an end," Monrad insisted. "We will have what is known as a *constitution monarchy* like Britain, the great power."

"We can continue this discussion later," Kristoffer replied. "I need to find my wife."

Monrad sighed and then said, "I recall her stating that she was going to go out and provide lunch for the tired workers at the mine."

"The mines! God in Heaven! The miners returned home from work hours ago and she still hasn't returned! My Klara… she must surely be in trouble. Do you know which mine she travelled to, old friend?"

Monrad thought for a moment and then nodded.

"The coal mines, my king," Monrad answered. "She said the coal mines."

"Very well," Kristoffer replied. "I will have to have my sleigh brought out so that I can go to the mines and look for my dear wife," he remarked. "I won't let anything happen to my Klara. Oh, my Klara, my entire world rests in her and her alone."

"Yes, sir," Kirk remarked. "Best of luck, my old king."

• •

Kristoffer stood in the courtyard as a sleigh pulled by two reindeer appeared from the gates. He added a belt around his waist with a sword in a holster. The sleigh was large and made of a darkened wood. It was painted on the side in a dark red with gold outlines. The tracks of the sleigh were made of mjolnium. There were two benches for seats in the front and rear. The sleigh made a loop around the courtyard before pulling up to the king. The man dressed in a similar apparel to the average worker but wearing a white wool coat and touphe jumped out and made space for the king to climb up.

"Wait!" a man shouted, rushing out of the castle.

Kristoffer turned over to the man, who appeared to be Lord Grundtvig. *Lord Grundtvig was another old friend of mine. He was a theologian and an inventor.* The lord had a grey beard and wore a similar suit to Lord Monrad, but in black.

"What is it, Kirk?" Kristoffer questioned.

"Sire, I just learned from Lord Monrad that you were going to the mines, and I must warn you that there was a terrible discovery there earlier today," Lord Grundtvig warned. "The miners said they uncovered a cavern of sort, which they asked that you not enter in case of the presence of trolls! If you believe your wife to be there, I urge that you be careful."

"I am not afraid of any troll, Kirk," Kristoffer replied.

"If you do not return, sire, what shall I do? Condemn the mine?"

"Nonsense," Kristoffer replied. "There will be no such failure. Do not worry and have faith in your king!"

"Sire..." Grundtvig attempted to interrupt.

"Heeyah," Kristoffer shouted, whipping the reins for the reindeer to rush forward.

The sleigh went forward on the snow and out of the castle, leaving Grundtvig behind. They passed through the outer courtyard and then came down a short bridge before going down a gentle road through the village. Various villagers looked out towards Kristoffer, stopping and stepping out of the way. Many of them, especially females, attempted to wave to him as they noticed their king passing by. The sleigh ran through the central plaza and then began to make its way towards the portcullis, which was open.

From the portcullis, the sleigh crossed over the bridge and then turned right to go towards the hills. In the distance of the hills was an observation tunnel and some huts. The sleigh made its approach towards both of them and then stopped outside of the entrance of a tunnel going into the hills. The portal into the mine was held by dark wooden logs. In front of the mine entrance was a wooden gate with tracks underneath and going outwards. There was a series of mine carts with coal loaded inside.

Kristoffer stepped out of the sleigh and then approached the gates. He opened the gates and then began to enter the darkened corridor, but not before taking a stick from a barrel and wrapping the stick with some cloth. He then went to a table where there were fire steels for him to use and light a fire from his torch.

With the torch in hand, he began to make his way into the mine alone. The walls of the cave were dark, and the tunnels were square-shaped. Kristoffer made it to the end of the primary tunnel as it started to dip downwards into the deeper depths of the hill. He slowly made his approach until he reached the lowest level. The walls were still dark, if not a darker shade of the rock of the island. A noticeable difference was the puddle of water that went to his ankles. The tunnel continued straight downwards with several intersections sprouting at either side every couple of hundred yards.

Once Kristoffer reached the end of the tunnel, he had the option of either going left or right, but instead of doing that, he went back around and chose a random tunnel to begin looking.

"Klara!" Kristoffer shouted. "Klara! Where are you, my love?!"

Kristoffer's voice echoed in the tunnels. There was no response. Kristoffer continued to wade through the knee-high water. He passed several more intersections and then turned around and looked around in confusion.

"Klara!" Kristoffer shouted, turning back around to go down the tunnel.

The water was now slowly rising up his thighs as he began to fasten his pace and become lost in the dark tunnels. Within another couple of minutes, it was at his waist and Kristoffer was violently shouting the name of his wife over and over as the water continued to rise and rise as the minutes passed and the fire on his torch blew out.

· ·

"I don't need to give you any more details of what happened," Kristoffer said to Charlemagne as they stood in the mines. "I remember everything now – I went out looking for her and came to this mine. I never did find her, and I suppose out of fright of what happened to me, nobody came to learn my fate until now."

Charlemagne and Kristoffer stood in the icy-walled tunnels of the mines with the kids, lit by flashlights.

"What now then?" Charlemagne questioned him.

"Now, if my wife was not in this mine, then there is only one other mine she could have gone to and that is our iron mine not too far from here. I will need to find boats to cross the waters and take those dogs out to cross the ice. I will find my wife, and we will resurrect this town. Together, we can bring a bright and cheerful Christmas to the children of Greenland once more."

"Together?" Charlemagne then questioned.

"Yes, together, for if I held the power to stay alive, then surely she must have too," Kristoffer explained. "I cannot allow that my wife has turned into a *draugr* at worst outcome. No. I know she is out there, waiting for me, and I will save her."

Act 5, Scene 1

Charlemagne stood by at the docks of Old Hvitrnord as Kristoffer and a couple of villagers pushed a longship into the water. The stern of the *drakkar* boat had the image of a dragon carved out. The sculpture was detailed and had a curved neck that led to ferocious teeth. In the center of the boat was a mast that went up with a folded sail. Rope attached to the top of the mast from either side of the boat: stern and bow. At the sides of the boat were about ten oars on each side. The boat that was pushed in the water matched another that had already been pushed in. Each of the boats were loaded with sleds in the center, while Kristoffer walked over to Lars.

"In my absence, I leave you in charge," Kristoffer stated to Lars. "See to it that all of the snow is cleared from the town of your ancestors, but do not concentrate all of your force into this project. Organize a team of your people's best hunters to take the spare boats out to hunt for food. My castle will be your home until the town is ready for the entire village and many more villagers of neighboring villages to move in. Hvitrnord used to be ten times the size and has room to grow. By the time I return, I expect to see the lively village I used to know. Do you understand this, Lord Jensen?"

"I do, my king," Lars replied. "Thank you, for everything you are doing. I have spoken with the others and we are all very hopeful that you are the savior we have hoped for. You will bring us into better times, my king."

"Of course," Kristoffer remarked. "Have an additional party visit the mines and begin to dig for coal. Use whatever surplus remains in the castle stores, but do not rely solely on this supply as it will run out fast."

"Yes, my king," Lars responded. "Best of luck on your journey."

Lars took a step back and then walked off. A group of four villagers remained to board the second longship alongside a pack of ten dogs. A second pack of ten dogs boarded the first ship. Kristoffer went to this first ship and entered the front. He then picked up an oar as Diana and Tristan walked over to Charlemagne who was still observing.

"Charles, what are we still doing around here?" Tristan asked. "Do we really need to help him find his wife?"

"I'm afraid we must if he is going to hand over some of his alien alloys," Charlemagne replied. "I cannot anger him. We simply have to help him realize his dream."

"His wife is dead," Tristan bluntly said. "There's no way she would have survived. You told me yourself, the only reason this dude survived under the ice was mostly likely because of his large size and thick coat."

Charlemagne turned to Tristan with a strict face.

"Do not let him hear you say that," Charlemagne warned. "Just stay and quiet – the two of you."

"What have I said?" Diana questioned in offense.

"Nothing," Charlemagne replied. "I'm only giving you a warning."

"Charlemagne!" Kristoffer shouted over to him. "What are you waiting for? My wife awaits me and you are just standing there?! Quickly, we must make off with haste!"

"Come along," Charlemagne said to the kids. "Let's go."

Charlemagne walked over to the longship and helped the kids aboard before climbing over the icy waters to get inside. Tristan looked into the water with fearful eyes. The surface of the water was dark, almost black due to the absence of light in the sky. The skies were still slightly cloudy, although it was clearing over in the north.

Kristoffer took the oars in the ship and began to push them forward, leading the second boat across the water with the other pack of dogs and villagers who were paddling along. Ahead of them, across the water was a sheet of thick ice that stretched for miles. The exposed water lasted between a kilometer or two. The longships floated downwards at a calm speed.

Diana kept her eyes on the water and Tristan maintained his focus forward. Once they were several meters inwards, Diana removed her camera from her backpack and brought the strap over his neck so she could try to take pictures of their surroundings. She hesitated between the scenery, focusing on the landscape, taking a picture here and there, but then looking around to see that there was nothing more. She sighed.

Tristan maintained a bored expression on his face. Diana looked to him. She saw his cold face and rosy-red nose. His skin was paler than its normal tone and she hadn't seen him like this since he fell in the ice cold water in Russia. Likewise, Tristan could see Diana's skin to be pure white like Kristoffer's and Charlemagne's, but of course, her skin was smooth and glowed. He smiled as he looked at her.

"How are you doing, Rudolph?" Diana asked.

"I'm alive," Tristan simply replied with a warm smile. "I'm almost missing the Ingstad a little and not constantly being cold."

"At least one day we can look back and say that we visited the Arctic – not quite the North Pole, but the Arctic," Diana said to him.

"Yeah," Tristan replied, widening his smile as he looked at her. "It's an experience."

"Perhaps that'll teach you both to not stowaway ever again," Charlemagne remarked to them as he produced a set of binoculars.

Diana and Tristan both looked over to him before shamelessly looking in the other direction. Charlemagne looked out in the opposite direction, towards the sea ice and scanned the horizon. All that existed was a flat plain of ice as he scanned from left to right. Charlemagne then adjusted the binoculars so that he could see even further. He then scanned from left to right, stopping in the middle of his scan.

At approximately fifteen miles from them was some sort of mound or rock in the ice. Charlemagne began to make note of the anomaly as he produced his old map and gave an approximate location based on where they were in the water as well as where Hvitrnord was. The anomaly was on the path towards the rogue island northwards.

Once Charlemagne was finished making a note of this item, he put his map away and continued to scan the horizons from left to right at increasing depths to the maximum of what would be possible at his altitude before putting his binoculars away. The longship was close to the coast and Kristoffer was making the last strokes before they could disembark.

The longship parked against the jagged ice horizontally and Kristoffer immediately set off planting spikes into the ice so that he could tie one of the boats and anchor it to the coast. By the time that was done, the second longship parked on the coast and the crew began to unload the second sled while Diana, Tristan, and Charlemagne unloaded the primary sled. The dogs slowly disembarked onto the ice one at a time until the sleds were ready and they were rushed onto the ice so that they could be prepared into their harnesses.

Once the two sleds were ready, Kristoffer looked to the villagers.

"Thank you for your aid," Kristoffer stated to the villagers in English. "Now, return home and work hard. We have lots of work to do before Christmas Day!"

The villagers got onto the second longship and pushed off from the coast to return to Hvitrnord. The coast of Greenland was barely visible through the fog that had built up despite the skies clearing.

Kristoffer turned to those that remained with him: Diana, Tristan, and Charlemagne.

"With all my reindeer dead, it looks like these dogs are all we have for transit. It'll do as long as we hurry," Kristoffer stated, going to one of the sleds. "Charlemagne, since you have the map, you lead us with your children."

"Of course," Charlemagne responded, going over to the sled. "Tristan, take the map and follow my directions."

Charlemagne handed Tristan the map. Tristan opened the map and noticed the path drawn. He then looked over to Charlemagne then Kristoffer. Charlemagne sat down at the lead of the primary sled as Diana sat behind him.

"Sure thing," Tristan replied, walking over to sit down in front of Diana.

"Onwards!" Kristoffer shouted.

Act 5, Scene 2

The dogs continued to march forward and forward into the Arctic Ocean. The fog dissipated as they went onwards and onwards, but a light wind began to pick up. They were currently in twilight, which gave them minimal light to see ahead of themselves. Within an hour of travel, Charlemagne could see with his naked eye the anomaly he previous spotted from the longship. It was large.

Kristoffer stopped his sled alongside Charlemagne as they looked over to the object. The two had agreed to investigate, so they continued and made their way over to the large object, which within another hour, appeared to be some sort of abandoned ship lodged in the ice, facing them from the starboard side. Tristan put the map away and simply laid back into Diana as they continued their trip over the sea ice towards this ship.

Several minutes past the second hour, Tristan could make out a flag at the bow of the ship at the jackstaff, a small vertical pole on the bow of the ship. It was a Soviet flag. However, the name of the side of the boat was explicitly not English, or rather, not in Cyrillic letters, but Roman letters. The name on the side of the boat stated the name, 'Ludendorff.'

"Well then," Charlemagne remarked as he read the name of the ship, "I suppose we've found where the Germans got to."

The Ludendorff was tilted at the stern with the bow slightly more above the ice. At the bow, behind the Soviet flag, was a large battery double-barreled gun pointed forward in front of the fore superstructure of the ship. Atop of the bridge was a large radar antennae composed in a three-dimensional cage grid. Behind this bridge was the main mast going towards an observation tower and upwards to where a German flag should be but wasn't. Immediately behind this mast was a smoke funnel followed by some space before another smoke funnel and then the aft superstructure. At the stern of the ship, there was simply a smaller gun pointed aft with railings that separated the boat from the ice behind the ship.

The sleds made their approach to the abandoned ship and stopped less than five yards from the bow. The ship was approximately two-hundred meters long and the hull of the ship at the bow was approximately ten meters tall. The hull had a hard chine, that is to say, the hull was angled with little rounding. Beneath the railings, on the immediate deck below the topside were portholes just as with the forward superstructure.

Kristoffer got off from his sled and stepped forward at the large size of the ship. He looked up and then over to Charlemagne.

"My Klara is here," Kristoffer stated. "I know it. She could be locked inside awaiting me to rescue her."

Charlemagne frowned for a moment as he looked to Kristoffer.

"Yes, well, perhaps we should have a moment to rest and let the dogs eat," Charlemagne instead said. "Once we've eaten, we can go in and investigate the interior of the ship."

"No time to lose," Kristoffer responded, taking with him a sack from his sled and slinging it around him. "I cannot wait any longer."

Kristoffer began to trek down the side of the ship towards the stern. Charlemagne looked over to the kids and sighed.

"Come on," Charlemagne said, "let's wait here and have some lunch. The dogs need to eat if we're going to get to that mine."

Tristan and Diana nodded and began to go through the backpacks on the sled. The dogs were fed from some tins of meat and gathered together. Twenty tins for twenty dogs. Tristan and

Diana opened each of them and set them out for the dogs before they had their own meals from some field rations taken from the Ingstad for them. Charlemagne picked up his ration package and then looked over to Kristoffer as he was halfway towards the stern of the boat. Charlemagne sighed and dropped his ration pack in his backpack.

"Christ, I better go and stay near him," Charlemagne remarked, picking up his backpack. "I don't want him to realize there's nothing here and then leave before I get the chance to explore. Stay here with the dogs, will you?"

"Aye," Tristan replied, watching as Charlemagne went off.

Charlemagne rushed forward along the side of the Ludendorff and watched as Kristoffer hopped over the railing of the boat. Charlemagne then walked faster so that he could get to the stern of the ship and bring himself over. Once over, he looked around for where Kristoffer had run off to and examined the ship.

The stern gun had icicles forming and drooping from the single barrel. The turret was covered in snow and the barrels were pointed slightly upwards. On either side behind the battery gun were a set of metal staircases going upwards a deck to the rest of the exterior of the ship. Behind this battery gun, on the next deck, was another gun just like the former and in front of the aft superstructure. The superstructure was only two stories tall. In front of the second story was a platform with an anti-air gun mounted and pointed upwards. Atop of the aft superstructure was a marine radar

Charlemagne climbed up a set of stairs and looked over to Kristoffer where he was attempting to bash into a watertight door with the side of his immense body. Kristoffer stopped as he saw Charlemagne approaching him.

"Good, you're here," Kristoffer said to him in a coarse voice. "The door is frozen shut."

"Stand by," Charlemagne said to him, taking off his backpack and setting it on the ground. "I can melt the ice around the sides."

Charlemagne rummaged around his bag and took out the blowtorch from earlier. He then turned it on and brought the flame to the perimeter of the watertight door. Charlemagne traced the flame around the edge and the ice melted into water that then dripped down to the ground. Once Charlemagne had made a lap, he turned off the flame and stepped out of the way for Kristoffer to bring himself into the door and cause it to swing open.

The pair then entered a cold corridor and proceeded down it. Charlemagne looked into the open doors next to them and saw washrooms where a series of toilets were lined up against the perimeter of the room. This room was next to another similar room, but with showers instead of toilets around the edge. Charlemagne produced a flashlight from his backpack and turned it on so that they had light.

At the end of the corridor was a set of metal stairs going into the depths of the boat. The pair travelled downwards and came into a simple corridor that extended aft and to the stern. Behind the staircase they had just come down was another one going further down. However, Kristoffer decided to go down the corridor of the deck. They walked downwards and looked into several rooms. One was a medical bay, which Charlemagne entered in search of supplies. There was very little left in some cabinets other than cloth and gauges. Against the wall of the medical bay were three stretcher-like beds followed by a desk and an office behind the desk. Charlemagne exited the room and continued down the corridor into the next room where Kristoffer was looking into. It was a simple room with a table in the middle and light fixtures hanging down.

The room next to this was a radio room with tables and chairs against the walls. Atop of the tables were large instruments with headsets connected into. The corridor then came to a watertight door after this room, which Kristoffer opened and then stepped into to see large crates of munitions stored about. The pair exited this space and went back where they came to go to the lower deck.

The staircase to the lower deck led into a large space with various berths – three of them stacked atop of each other spread about the open space. Charlemagne and Kristoffer walked forward along the aisles of the berthing area to come to some mess tables with ten chairs at each table. Behind the mess area was a wall with two watertight doors at either end. Kristoffer opened the first and entered a small kitchen. Behind the kitchen was another door that came into a storage room with various crates of food lying around. Kristoffer's eyes widened as he saw the crates. He then proceeded to attempt to open one but was unable to with his hands. He eyed an axe nearby and took it. He then swung it down to open a crate.

The opened crate released a pungent odor that causes Charlemagne to step out of the way.

"Damn," Kristoffer remarked, looking inside.

Kristoffer then exited the room and closed the door behind him. He then went out of the kitchen and around to the other watertight door, which led into another washroom with a second door in the back going into a shower room. Charlemagne looked to Kristoffer as he closed the door. Kristoffer then proceeded to return the way they came.

The two returned to the top deck and exited outside. They then proceeded to walk down the side of the ship, passing torpedo tubes that were tucked away behind one of the smoke funnels. Behind the smoke funnel were three lifeboats stacked upon each other behind the forward superstructure. The duo came around to the watertight door into this space and Charlemagne knelt down to melt the ice around the perimeter of the door. Kristoffer then opened the door and they stepped into a corridor that went that cut into a T-intersection before going through the middle of the deck.

At each side were doors entering small bedrooms. Each bedroom had a single bed with a toilet in the corner and desk at the opposite side. At the end of the hallway was a staircase on the left and radio room on the right. The two went upwards a level, which came into a smaller space with two bedrooms ahead and a larger radio room on the left. Charlemagne shined his light and then followed Kristopher to the next level. The foyer of this room was small. On the left was a door entering the combat information center, which had a table in the center with various chairs spread out. There was a map on the wall behind this table and a desk with a panel and various dials and buttons.

The room ahead of them was the steering-station, which was much smaller than the one on the Ingstad. It was also not that different. The two walked into the bridge and looked out of the large windows, which were covered in frost and impossible to see through. In the middle was a steering wheel and to the left of the wheel was a table with charts. Immediately in front of them was a classical telegraph with the lever pointed in the middle. The pair exited the room and returned to the foyer to go up another level, which came to a hatch. Kristopher attempted to push through the hatch, but it was closed, so they went down all the way to where they had come from to go down into the bowels of the ship again.

The first deck below was similar to the aft of the ship, but instead of a medical bay, there was instead a workshop with various tools including a work bench, drill press, lathe, bench grinder, and some welding equipment. The workshop led into an office presumed to belong to the former engineer. The room next to this, going towards the bow, were some lavatories and shower rooms before going into a mechanical room with a windlass in the middle and some piping around. The pair then turned around and went back to the staircase to go aft where they passed another mechanical room where the uptake ducts of the aft smoke funnel passed through and then another workshop to their right followed by a watertight door ahead of them at the end of the corridor.

Kristoffer turned the valve of the watertight door and came into a large empty room that stretched the entire width of the ship and went aft for about five meters. Charlemagne shined his light into the room and then went into the workshop and shined his light at diagrams on the walls of the space.

"These don't look like they have anything to do with this ship..." Charlemagne whispered to himself as he looked at these complicated schematics. "What's more curious is the lack of the dead on this boat..."

Charlemagne looked at the schematics with careful eyes. They looked to be like the schematics of a smaller boat or type of submarine. The problem, however, was that the bird's-eye view of the item was circular. The anterior and posterior view of this object was cigar-shaped.

"Karl!" Kristopher shouted from the other room.

Charlemagne exited and entered the empty space. He shined his light over to where Kristoffer was. He was in the far right corner of the room, examining a small device on the wall.

Charlemagne walked over and looked at it. There was a slit in the middle of the rectangular panel.

"Looks as though a key could fit inside," Charlemagne remarked, bringing his finger over the keyhole. "Hm…"

Charlemagne shined his light towards the wall and stepped towards it. Like in Egypt, he brought his hands to the wall and began to feel around for a slit. He brought his nails across and stopped at the far-side opposite from Kristoffer.

"There's something behind this wall," Charlemagne remarked.

"Klara!" Kristoffer suggested, raising his axe.

"Possibly," Charlemagne simply replied. "We need to find the key…"

"I'm coming my love!" Kristoffer instead said, bringing the axe down onto the hard metal.

Kristoffer created a hole in the wall and he continued to dig into the shutter like a madman. Charlemagne simply stood back and watched in horror as Kristoffer dug into the hole he had made, pulling at the door and eventually causing it to rise upwards and inwards into a room behind. Charlemagne shined his light inside and instead of Kristoffer's wife, they found a small arsenal of robots standing side-by-side with *Sturmgewehr 44* (StG 44) rifles at their sides. The robots were split into two small platoons that faced each other. Charlemagne stepped forward and looked at the robots, shining his light at them.

The faces of the robots were skull-like and they had chiseled teeth at the front of their face with dark and empty eye sockets or orbits. Their faces were anatomically correct and extremely detailed to fine degree. The figures had no nose, but a space over the nose and at the cheeks were additional spaces that looked inside of the skull of this creature.

Red wires extended downward from the skull like veins into the torso piece. Thin plates existed where the pectoral muscles would be. There was no rib cage, but there was a spine that went down to a pelvis. The robot had shoulder sockets extending above the chest and joined together like a clavicle bone. Protruding from these sockets and outwards was a thick metal humerus that connected to a conjoined ulna and radius. This particular robot had no hands.

The femur of the robot was thicker than the humerus and connected to a socket at the pelvis and another socket at the knee. Like the hands, there were no feet, but there was a conjoined tibia and fibula. Around the limb bones were a mesh of thick wires and corrugated tubes.

Charlemagne looked around the room and walked down the middle of the aisle between the two platoons of robots. He then reached the end where there were watertight doors on either side. He walked over to one and began to open one of the valves. The room on the other side was a mechanical room with the uptake ducts of the aft smoke funnel, but on the outer edge was a workbench with diagrams strewn around. Charlemagne rushed over to the diagrams and shined his light on them – they were in relation to the robots in the other room. Kristoffer entered at the doorway and stood there as Charlemagne looked at the diagrams.

"*Panzerknacker,*" Charlemagne read in the corner. "Tank busters. Good grief…"

Charlemagne studied the blueprints with intent, squinting his eyes as he read the German writing and then looked over to Kristoffer.

"Whoever designed these was immensely ahead of his time. The Germans were infamous for that during the war…" Charlemagne remarked. "It's a shame really."

"Karl…" Kristoffer simply said to him in a more mournful voice.

"What is it?" Charlemagne questioned, relaxing his eyes.

Kristoffer had his finger pointed forward. Charlemagne looked at him and then turned around. He shined his light and saw the mummified remains of a man hanging by a noose tied to a pipe in the ceiling. The man's skin was sickly pale and almost blue from where he had hanged their dead in the cold. His face was lifeless. The appearance of the corpse was like a prop, but its features were organic and natural. He was half-dressed in a *Schutzstaffel* uniform with only his boots and trousers being from the uniform and his top being an undershirt.

Charlemagne looked at the corpse in horror and then turned aside. Kristoffer walked over and with his axe, cut the man down and brought the body to the ground.

"A proper funeral awaits this man," Kristoffer stated. "We shall build him a *bål* and burn him."

Charlemagne kept his back turned away from the corpse and looked at the bench where he saw a book. He picked it up and looked inside. It was a journal and beside it was a German-made pistol known as a Walther P38. Charlemagne skimmed through the book and read the last entry.

"The boat was raided by the Russians…" Charlemagne stated. "He was left behind and was stuck with the entire ship damaged. He chose to end his life rather than starve in the cold."

The two of them looked out the door as they heard some howling coming from outside.

"The dogs!" Kristoffer remarked.

"The kids!" Charlemagne added.

"We must go at once!" Kristoffer then said, rushing past Charlemagne to exit.

Act 5, Scene 3

Diana and Tristan ate from their ration packs outside in the cold as they waited for Kristoffer and Charlemagne to return. Charlemagne had just vanished from Tristan's sight when Diana nudged him.

"I'll trade you your crackers for my cookies," Diana offered him.

Tristan looked down into his ration pack and picked up the packet of four round crackers given to him. He then traded them for the two thick cookies in Diana's packet. The couple continued to eat their lunches when Tristan looked to the side and noticed a dog attempting to get free from his leash.

The dog, one with yellow hair, was separate from the rest of the dogs who were eating away. He held his head down to the ice and with his paw, attempted to remove his collar from his neck. The collar was loose and slid off with ease. Once the collar was off, the dog trotted off and away from the pack to the other side of the boat. Diana and Tristan both set their food onto the ice as they saw the dog run away from them and ran after the dog. The dog barked as it ran away and came to the other side.

Diana and Tristan followed and reached the other side of the boat, noticing a large hole in the side of the hull on the portside. The hole led into a small, but empty cargo hold where snow poured in from the outside. The dog ran into the ship and then went towards an open watertight door.

"Hey, stop!" Tristan called out to the dog, but he was already gone.

Diana and Tristan entered the ship and proceeded to chase the dog into the next room. The couple stopped upon entering and stared around the darkness that surrounded them. Tristan produced a flashlight from his backpack and shined it around.

The flashlight was bright and lit a decent amount of space around them, which was a large and tall spacious room with tanks lined against the perimeter wall in three columns of three. In between each column were elevated platforms reached by three steps. Around the perimeter of the room were further elevated catwalks that wrapped around. The dog hopped onto the platforms surrounding the tanks and began to rush down to the end of the room and through another watertight door.

Tristan turned around as he entered this tank room and closed the door behind them.

"We'll trap him room by room," Tristan said to Diana. "So he can't get out."

"Tristan, we just left the other dogs on their own," Diana complained.

"Relax, they'll be fine," Tristan responded. "It's not like we've seen any predators – let's go get that dog!"

The couple rushed up the steps and down to the next watertight door, which led into a crowded, but similar room. Immediately upon entering, they met another raised platform led to by a three step staircase. The room had a variety of pipes along the walls and was split into two sections on each side, starboard and port. On the portside, which they were on now, there was a small diesel generator in the middle and two more generators on either side ahead of them, blocking any progression further into the ship. The platform they stood on was split into two on this side of the room. There was a single bridge that connected the two sides of this section and two bridges in front of and behind the generator in the middle of the two sections. On the right were medium-sized tanks. The room was short – only approximately twenty meters in length. In front of them was a staircase going upwards.

"There," Tristan pointed, pointing behind the generator in the middle of the room.

Diana followed the dog into the starboard side of the room where there was a large cylindrical tank standing up and in the middle going into the room above with platform surrounding the edge. The platform led to a watertight door to the next room. The tank had the word *Kessel* across the front in large white font. The dog went through with Diana and Tristan following not too far from behind into the next room. The next room was similar on either side with two large and long engines on either section and surrounded by platforms. This room was similarly sized compared to the last one. It had a surrounding platform on the next level with a space in the middle looking down at the diesel engines.

Two watertight doors exited on either side, but only the one on the left, the starboard side, was open. The dog was seen running into the next room and the couple followed. The next room was like the former, but opposite. A large tank exited in front of them and on the starboard side there were various machines. Beneath them, in the middle of each section was a long cylindrical shaft that extended through the entire floor. There were, however, motors at the end of the room and a single door around the large tank on the portside. The dog entered this room and came into the aft engine room, which was like the forward engine room, but with only one pair of engines on the portside. From here, the dog crossed to the other side.

Diana and Tristan came into this room, which was similar in appearance to the initial room with three columns of tanks surrounded by a platform and a catwalk around the perimeter. Tristan rushed up the steps onto the platform and then sprinted down to reach the dog as it was going into the next open doorway. The dog slipped through with Tristan behind him and came into the next room with him. It then stopped not too far into the room and let out a lone bark. Tristan came towards the dog and grabbed it by the stomach, letting go of his lantern on the floor and picking the dog up before then looking forward in slight fear.

The room they had entered was a cargo hold like at the bow of the ship, except this one was slightly longer with a similar catwalk around the perimeter. There were various crates around, but towards the corner of the room cozied between some wooden crates was a large white creature curled up and sleeping. It was a polar bear deep in its slumber with its belly facing towards Tristan. The bear was approximately two meters in length and was large and fluffy. Its fur was cream-colored and it had smaller bears at its teat. She was a mother.

Diana caught up to Tristan and looked into the room. She saw the bear and picked up the flashlight on the floor.

"I think we should leave," Tristan suggested, taking a step back.

"Good idea," Diana replied, walking with him so they could be out of sight.

The couple exited the cargo hold and came into the aft fuel tank room. They proceeded to walk back towards the engine room with Diana holding the light and Tristan carrying the large dog in his arms. They entered the rear of the engine room and began to walk down the aisle between two engines before stopping as they heard the sound of some metal moving on the floor around. The two came to the end of the aisle and peaked into the starboard side of the aft engine room. The couple then froze.

The dog in Tristan's arm growled and then gave off a loud bark. It pulled away from Tristan's arm and ran towards the even larger polar bear that stood before them on all fours. The bear returned noise and gave off a ferocious roar, which caused the dog to yelp and run away.

"No!" Tristan shouted as the dog ran off.

The polar bear ahead of the couple was approximately double the size of the former they had seen. Its fur was whiter and its head was approximately the size of a yoga ball. The bear marched towards the pair, which caused Diana to take Tristan's hand.

"Tristan, let's go," Diana cautioned, pulling him away.

The bear came towards them as they ran into the aft boiler room. They ran around the large boiler and towards the open watertight door into the aft engine room. From here, they crossed into the aft boiler room and then into the fuel tank room. The polar bear was right behind them and navigating around the machinery in the tight space. The couple went up the three steps of the fuel tank platforms and they ran down towards the watertight door only to stop as Tristan had closed it prior.

Tristan immediately proceeded to turn the valve while Diana watched from behind as the polar bear stomped towards them.

"No time," Diana cautioned, pulling Tristan away from the door. "Come here."

Diana climbed up a ladder near them to go towards the catwalk. Tristan looked at the bear increasingly getting close and did the same. The polar bear stood up on its feet as Tristan climbed over and onto the platform. The height of the bear was immense and almost ten feet tall. It could bring its hands right to the edge of the catwalk, which caused the couple to back away and hug the outer wall.

"Christ," Tristan remarked. "What the hell do we do?"

"There must be another way out," Diana reasoned. "How else are people above supposed to get down here?"

"True," Tristan replied.

The polar bear began to shake the catwalk platform to the couple's dismay. Tristan began to sneak around to the corner so they could use the platform to go around to the other watertight door into the forward cargo hold. The door was open and led into the catwalk of the forward cargo hold. However, he stopped as he saw two sections of the catwalk break apart and the platform dip downwards slightly due to the tremors. Tristan immediately grabbed the railing and felt his boot tapped by the paw of the polar bear. He backed off and led Diana around. They then ran down the platform and went aft, coming to a watertight door that was locked and closed.

Tristan began to turn the valve. It was rusted and difficult to turn, but he was able to unlock the door and open it. The couple then disappeared into the forward boiler second level, which led into an open space with cabinets similar to the ones in the Ingstad engine control room lined up near a table. Tristan closed the door behind him. There were railings around the opening in the floor that allowed the boiler to rise up. Diana shined the light around the room in search of an exit way, but they couldn't find anything.

The couple could hear the sound of metal banging around in the fuel tank room behind them. They finished their search and then came to a watertight door going into the forward engine room. Tristan turned it and then the two entered, closing the door behind them as well. The second level of the engine room simply had railings around the openings that looked down to the engines. There was, however, a set of stairs that went upwards.

Tristan rushed towards the stairs, but stopped as he saw the lost dog appear from an open watertight door between the second level of the aft boiler room and forward engine room.

"Hey!" Tristan shouted, going around to the dog.

The dog woofed at him as he picked him up.

"Come on, let's get out of here," Tristan said, going back over to the ladder stairs.

Tristan looked at Diana as the three reunited.

"I think that polar bear is trapped," Tristan said to her.

"It better be," Diana remarked. "We left nineteen dogs outside undefended otherwise."

The two went up the stairs and came into a dark open area with tables around them and then berths on the other side. They walked down and saw a set of stairs going upwards at the end. Tristan held the dog in his arms as he went up the stairs. Once at the top, the couple froze as they heard the howls of the dogs outside.

"Uh oh," Tristan said to Diana.

"Hurry," Diana replied, rushing up the steps.

The couple stopped as they saw the flash of a lantern at the other side of the corridor. It was Charlemagne's flashlight with Kristoffer sprinting down the corridor.

"*Ikke hundene!*" Kristoffer yelled, going up the stairs.

The kids looked to Charlemagne as he reached them. He simply gave them a look and then went up the way that Kristoffer had went. The children followed him and came out to the starboard side of the weather deck (top-side). Charlemagne ran outside and looked to the left as he saw Kristoffer sprinting forward to the bow of the ship. He ran after him and witnessed Kristoffer raised his axe up and then jump over the side of the ship and to the ice below.

Charlemagne stopped at the railing and looked down at the sight of Kristoffer hugging a polar bear from behind and using his axe to choke the bear at his neck. The kids caught up with Tristan still carrying the lost dog.

"Good grief!" Charlemagne remarked as he saw the bear on its hind legs, walking backwards and shouting as he tried to shake Kristoffer off.

"Do something!" Diana pleaded.

"What am I to do?" Charlemagne questioned. "I can't fight a bear any more than he can!"

The polar bear eventually knocked Kristoffer and caused him to slide away. He quickly got to his feet and the two faced each other. Kristoffer then ran towards the bear like a mad man.

"Hold on," Charlemagne stated, stepping back. "I *can* do something."

Charlemagne disappeared, leaving the kids to watch with the dogs barking in the background. Kristoffer drop kicked pass the bear's left-side, swinging his axe at one of its legs and causing it to come down on all fours. He then brought the axe down over back of the bear, which caused it to rise up again and punch Kristoffer across the face.

"Oh my God," Tristan remarked.

The polar bear caused Kristoffer to collapse onto the floor. He then went over to him and stomped his feet down, but Kristoffer rolled out of the way and picked up his axe. He then gave himself some distance from the bear as the two faced each other again. The bear was bleeding heavily from its back and left leg. Tristan had just noticed blood to be dripping from Kristoffer's left hand.

The polar bear and the viking paced around each other. The polar bear was limping. Kristoffer then charged at the bear, causing it to stand up and swing an arm at him. Kristoffer ducked. The bear swung again. He ducked once more but was knocked backwards. The polar bear then moved to stomp down, but Kristoffer rolled out of the way and backed off.

Charlemagne finally returned, wielding a StG 44 and came to the railing of the ship. He looked over to the bear as it was about to sprint towards Kristoffer. Charlemagne cocked the weapon and opened fire at the bear, hitting it in its right torso. The bear shouted in pain. Kristoffer jumped out of the way and collapsed on the ground. The bear too collapsed on the ice and slid about two meters. It lay on its side as Kristoffer stood up and went over to the bear. He raised the axe and swung it down onto the neck of the bear, killing it instantly with a single strike.

Diana closed her eyes into Tristan's torso, but Tristan watched. Kristoffer raised the axe again and made another swing, decapitating the bear and then tossing the head down. He collapsed onto the ground and sat against the body of the bear. He panted. Charlemagne lowered the rifle and looked down. He then looked over to the kids and gave off a sigh. Kristoffer proceeded to examine his wounds, which seemed superficial.

"Karl, if you could be so kind, bring me some bandage so I can fix myself up..." Kristoffer shouted from below. "We don't have much time. We have to get moving again!"

Act 5, Scene 4

Kristoffer tossed some wooden planks found from within the Ludendorff onto the pyre he had created on the stern of the ship. Charlemagne watched with a hand inside his jacket. He then looked inside his coat and at the pistol he had taken from the workshop. He kept it inside an inner pocket and then retreated his hand so that he could look over to Kristoffer with crossed arms. Kristoffer carried the body over to the pyre and placed it atop. He then stepped back and took off his hat.

"Mr. Cabernet, if you would please light the fire," Kristoffer requested.

"Yes," Charlemagne responded, taking out his blowtorch and walking over to the pyre.

Charlemagne lit the flame from the base of the pyre and then stepped back as the fire spread until they had a medium-sized bonfire. The two watched the corpse burn until it became charred. Afterwards, they stepped off the boat and proceeded to walk back to the kids and the dogs. Charlemagne frowned as he saw Tristan fooling around with the assault rifle at Kristoffer's sled with Diana fixing the collar of the dog that had ran off.

Kristoffer had loaded both the rifle and the carcass of the polar bear onto his sled.

"Tristan, put that down," Charlemagne said in a strict voice. "It is not a toy."

"Sorry…" Tristan remarked, gently putting it back onto the sled.

"Have you opened the door you closed so that mother polar bear can exit in the springtime?" Charlemagne then questioned.

"Yes, sir," Tristan responded.

"Good lad," Charlemagne replied.

Kristoffer walked over to his sled and patted the polar bear he had caught.

"We will eat well on the Christmas Day, my friends," Kristoffer boasted. "The meat of a polar bear is the meat of royalty. The fur will make a nice coat!"

Charlemagne nodded and then took out a map as well as a compass. He began to make notes on the back of the map and then looked around. The kids sat down in the sled. Charlemagne sat down in front of them and without further ado, they left.

• •

From the Ludendorff, the sleds travelled a couple of kilometers north along barren lands before they could see a small rock in the distance. The small rock was larger than it initially appeared and according to Kristoffer, was the site of the iron mine set up short into his reign. The sleds pulled towards the mine and then stopped outside of what appeared to be a wooden portal covered by wooden doors.

The wooden doors were frosted over and locked by an iron chain around the handles. Kristoffer got off from his sled and went over to the door. He took his axe and broke the chain, tossing it aside and then entering alone. Charlemagne stood up from his sled and turned to the kids.

"Wait here, and please don't lose any of the dogs," Charlemagne requested.

"Sure thing," Tristan replied.

Charlemagne went after Kristoffer into the depths of the mine. Kristoffer stopped a couple of meters inside as he realized it was too dark for him to go in alone. Charlemagne took out his flashlight and provided some light. The ground was composed of loose rock around the tracks. The two walked a couple of meters forward before the tunnel began to delve downwards.

The tunnel began to level out as they went forward. Charlemagne continued to shine his light into the darkness. Within a couple of meters on the next level, the two could see something along the left wall. It looked to be a medium-sized person lying on the left wall with an arm under the head as if they had laid there to go to sleep.

"Klara!" Kristoffer shouted, rushing forward. *"Klara! Klara! Min dejlige Klara!"*

Kristoffer brought his hands to his wife's torso and began to shake her. Her body was hardened and her skin was blue. Her eyes were closed. Charlemagne kept his distance and watched from where he was.

"Karl, help her! Help her like you helped me!" Kristoffer pleaded.

Charlemagne looked at the two and then walked forward. He set his backpack down and retrieved the blowtorch. He then looked at Klara who had snow white hair and appeared to be quite young – in her late thirties. Her skin was flawless and she existed now in a state of incorruptibility.

"Karl? What are you waiting for?" Kristoffer asked.

"She's dead," Charlemagne confessed. "I can't do anything to save her. Unlike you, your wife does not have the mass to have survived frozen for over eighty years. I'm sorry."

"Don't be mad!" Kristoffer shouted at him. "Is it not possible?"

"I'm sorry, it's not, and if I defrost the layer of ice around her, then her body will most likely begin to decay. I do not think you want that – as she is, she is as she was."

Charlemagne finally looked over to Kristoffer. The sides of his eyes were wet with tears that had fallen down. Charlemagne put the blowtorch away, picked up his backpack and stood up. He then moved aside as Kristoffer knelt over and proceeded to cry with his body over his wife. His crying turned to him shouting as the man let out. He then picked the body of his wife up with both arms and proceeded to carry her down to the end of the tunnel, which was not too far from where they were. He set her down against the wall directly in front of them and continued to cry.

Kristopher continued to cry and eventually Charlemagne decided to leave, dropping the lantern on the ground for Kristoffer and turning on a smaller spare to guide himself out.

The kids looked to Charlemagne as he exited from the mine. Charlemagne didn't have a proud smile on his face. Instead, it was somber.

"What happened?" Tristan asked as Charlemagne walked to them.

"What do you think, Tristan? Kristoffer's realized that his wife is dead," Charlemagne confessed, taking a sigh. "There was no chance of her being alive – none whatsoever."

"What now?" Diana then asked.

"I've marked the coordinates of that abandoned ship on my map. The robots inside the ship were made of the material I need. I'll see to it that we can recover them to salvage the alloy. Other than that, I believe we should be returning to the Ingstad soon."

"I want to go back to the boat and look for a souvenir to take with me – I haven't been able to find anything but ice around here," Diana complained.

"We're not pirates, Diana," Charlemagne scolded, "and you can't keep the assault rifle either."

Diana groaned and then replied, "What about you? You're looting all of those robots…"

"I'm recovering them… for scientific purposes…" Charlemagne rationalized. "Besides, there was nothing in the ship worth stealing… although, the entire site was a wonder."

Charlemagne proceeded to explain in depth what he found in the workshop – the blueprints on the wall that resembled a spacecraft of some sort. In addition, he explained to them in depth the details of the robots and the journal he found, which explained how Soviets had stalled the ship in the ice and then boarded to massacre all of the crew. He then told them of the fate of the corpses, how the Soviets had dug into the ice and thrown all of them underwater like a mass grave.

"What I find most curious," Charlemagne said, "is the relationship between these robots and the ones found in Russia. My guess is that the Russians stole the design off of the Germans as they did with many other projects."

Charlemagne stopped speaking as he heard footsteps behind him. He turned around and looked over to Kristoffer who had exited the tomb with the flashlight and set it on the ground. He began to close the doors to the mine before going to his sled.

"Kristoffer," Charlemagne said to him.

"What," Kristoffer replied in a sunken state.

"What of Klara?" Charlemagne asked.

"To rest in her final resting place," Kristoffer replied in an emotionless voice. "Come, we have work to do in Hvitrnord."

Kristoffer sat down at his sled and then whipped the dogs to go. Charlemagne looked at the kids and sat down. They promptly followed him back to the shore.

Act 6, Scene 1

Kristoffer disembarked from his longship and immediately set off from the docks. Charlemagne and the kids took their time to unload the dogs from each boat and have them follow them back to the castle. The village was still for the most part covered in a thick layer of snow that was almost two stories high. They navigated through and came to the hill to the castle. From the castle, once inside the inner courtyard, Charlemagne turned to the kids, giving his leash of ten dogs to Diana.

"Take these dogs to their room and get them fed," Charlemagne instructed. "I'm going to go speak to Kristoffer."

"Are we going to leave tomorrow?" Diana asked.

"I'm not sure," Charlemagne responded. "I don't know if we're going to be leaving soon... I don't want to leave Kristoffer nor these townspeople alone just yet."

Diana looked to Tristan. The two then shrugged as Charlemagne ran off and went inside. Charlemagne walked up to the Kristoffer's bedroom and knocked on the door.

"What is it?" Kristoffer asked from the other side.

"It's Charlemagne – can I come in?" Charlemagne asked.

No response came. Charlemagne opened the door and entered to see Kristoffer sat on his bed. Charlemagne closed the door behind him.

"I can see that you're sad, but I must ask what you intend to do next," Charlemagne said to him. "For the sake of your people and yourself."

"My wife was a woman who never upset anyone, Karlmann," Kristoffer said. "She was loved by the people and she loved them. She never disappointed anyone. She didn't deserve to die in that mine – alone. I should have come and rescued her, but instead, I went to the wrong mine."

"It's typical to blame yourself for the loss of those you love, but it does not resolve anything," Charlemagne said to him. "It does not bring them back from the dead. All you can do with that guilt is to make improvements of yourself to let that person never die in your heart."

"Yes…" Kristoffer confessed. "Klara will not die out. No, instead, the love of my wife will echo forever. To my people, I will give them the happiest Christmas of their lives and we will work together for the good of the entire world."

Charlemagne was silent and held a face as if he wanted to interrupt.

Kristoffer stood up and put both hands on Charlemagne's shoulder. He continued to hold a mournful face.

"I need some time alone to recover from this loss," Kristoffer stated. "In the meantime, could you please guide my people with your leadership experience. Turn these medieval ruins into the thriving town it once was. The people look onto you as they look onto me. Bring smiles onto their faces – now go!"

Kristoffer led Charlemagne to the doorway out of his room.

"Very well," Charlemagne responded to Kristoffer, "but I cannot stay any longer. I will stay until Christmas Day and then I'm afraid I'll have to be on my way."

"It's a deal, Mr. Cabernet. Now please, go!" Kristoffer insisted, opening the door. "You have much work to do tomorrow."

Kristoffer led Charlemagne out of his room. He then closed the door behind him. Charlemagne looked back at the door, gave a sigh, and then walked down the steps to return to the kids.

Act 6, Scene 2

The next morning, Charlemagne sat on his bed, counting the number of ration meals that were left for him and the kids. There were approximately twelve left in his own backpack, which meant the kids had twelve each in their backpacks as well. Charlemagne put his rations back into his backpack and then jumped at the sound of knocking on his door. He quickly put the food packs away and stood up to go to the door. He opened it and saw Lars standing.

"Hello," Lars greeted. "Are you ready, Mr. Cabernet?"

"For?" Charlemagne asked.

"To lead us," Lars simply responded. "We have not made much progress in the last day and the days are short, and there is much we are incapable of doing to meet his demands."

"Okay... what have you started on doing?" Charlemagne asked, crossing his arms.

"We tried to clean the streets, but there is too much snow and we do not know where to put it all. We sent two teams to do some fishing, but there is little in the sea to catch and some of the men came down with some food poisoning after cooking some of the fish last night. Lastly, we went to the mine but were unable to start any of the machines."

"Right..." Charlemagne replied sighing, "well, how about we go to the mine and I can take a look at the machinery and then we go to the docks so I can see about the fishing."

"Yes, Mr. Cabernet."

Charlemagne fetched his coat and then left his bedroom with Lars. The two exited the castle and left the castle ground to go downhill to the village. At the base of the village, they met the four-meter tall wall of snow that some villagers were attempting to clear out. Behind the wall were piles of snow from what they had managed to clear out. Additionally, there were two sleighs parked nearby filled with snow.

"As you can see, we have made little progress with the snow," Lars pointed out. "Worst of all, we have nowhere to put the snow."

"I see," Charlemagne responded, putting his hands in his pockets. "If only you had some sort of machine to clear out this snow, that would be useful…"

"Yes!" Lars replied. "It would be useful."

"Hm…" Charlemagne thought aloud. "And you can't inhabit the abandoned houses until then, well, you'll have to continue as you are, but perhaps begin from the village gate and remove the snow into the fjord. There is ample space there and when the ice melts in the summer, it'll become part of the ocean."

"Good idea," Lars replied.

Lars then spoke to the men in Danish. Charlemagne looked on and then looked around. He gave a sigh and then looked to Lars and then the men. The men looked disheartened and worn out already. All Charlemagne could do was give them his pity. The tour continued uphill and towards the path carved out in the snow to go to the mines.

Once at the mines, Charlemagne looked over to the half-dozen men sitting around. They all stood up upon seeing Charlemagne.

"Right, show me what's wrong in the mines," Charlemagne said, stopping in front of the gates.

Lars began to open the gates and then the two walked into the mines, coming down to the ice caverns where certain portions of the walls closest to the entrance had been chipped at and exposed. The walls were simply empty rock. The tour went to the end of the cave where Charlemagne was brought to a large machine.

The machine had a wide body with a long neck going towards a double-headed buzz saw pointed at the black wall in front of them. Charlemagne gave a quick look at the machine and attempted to figure out how to start it. He then looked over to Lars and three miners that were looking at him.

"Right, well, it doesn't appear to be broken," Charlemagne said to them. "Do any of you know how to start it?"

Lars and the others simply shrugged.

"Right... well, for a start you'll need to bring some coal down here as well as fill this boiler with some water. From there, you burn the coal, heating up the water and creating steam, which will cause pistons to move and turn the wheels, including the frontal saws. You simply need to push the vessel into the wall to get it to dig through the coal."

"But Mr. Cabernet," Lars interrupted. "We already started the machine once, but the wheels wouldn't turn. Our problem is in getting the wheels to turn."

"Oh..." Charlemagne responded. "Hm, then perhaps it is broken then. I'll need to take a look at the pistons. They may be rusted or something. In the meantime, have the men take some pickaxes to dig into the rock ahead as well as to clear the ice on the rails. We'll need to use these rails to transport materials from the surface to down here."

"Yes, Mr. Cabernet," Lars responded, turning to the men to talk to them in Danish.

Charlemagne watched and witnessed the men being sarcastic and bitter with Lars. Lars then turned to Charlemagne.

"Right, let's go to the docks now, shall we?" Charlemagne asked.

Act 6, Scene 3

Charlemagne and Lars began to walk out of the mines and then stepped out into the twilight-lit outdoors.

"Thank you, Mr. Cabernet, for your help," Lars said to him.

"Please, no thanks is necessary," Charlemagne sighed. "Most of your troubles – or rather, most of Kristoffer's troubles could be solved with modern technology that isn't available to us right now. He asks a lot of your people, and I'm sorry for that."

Charlemagne and Lars travelled across town to the docks of Hvitrnord where another half-dozen men were sitting around on crates by the docks. The boats sat in the water, moored to the docks. Charlemagne and Lars walked down the side of the docks to come to a shack. Lars opened the doors and inside they looked at the various fish that had been caught. There was about four in total.

"Two of the men had fallen ill when they had one of these fishes here," Lars stated. "I am not sure which of these it was, but we have known for a while that the waters have been contaminated to eat from."

"That is troubling," Charlemagne responded, walking into the shed and looking at each fish.

One of the fishes present had three dorsal fins and two ventral fins. It was brownish in color and less than a meter in length. The second fish was fatter and had two dorsal fins and three ventral fins. It was shaped like a salmon, but was not ray-finned. It also had whiskers. The third fish was a flounder – it was flat, but not as flat as the fourth fish, which was a halibut.

"I'll have to take samples of each of these fish and run some simple tests for toxicity," Charlemagne stated. "In fact, I have to do the same with that polar bear. The Arctic is known to have various PCBs in its waters – I'll also test the waters to see what is there as well. Until then, refrain from eating anything from the waters for the health of the men. Do you have any rations from your homes?"

"Yes, but our stocks are dwindling and most of them cannot be heated on the stoves in the kitchen," Lars complained as Charlemagne walked over to him. "What else can we do?"

"Well, the only other option would be to set up hunting parties – I'm sure Kristoffer would be open to that. There are caribou, or reindeer, in these parts of the land and there should also be seals. Then again, seals might carry the same toxins as these fish, but in greater numbers. You see, the higher an animal is on a food chain, the greater the concentration of heavy metals and other toxins in the fatty tissues of these animals. It is a process known as biomagnification."

Charlemagne sighed.

"Have you seen caribou in these parts?"

Lars shook his head.

Charlemagne gave another sigh. The two came out of the shed and went towards the water. He looked behind him and saw some empty glass bottles lying around, so he went over to one and picked it up. He then went back to the edge of the dock and filled the bottle with some of the ocean water. He looked at the water and then stood up.

"What are you going to do to help us?" a man asked from behind in a thick Danish accent.

Charlemagne turned around and looked over to the man. He was young, perhaps in his thirties with medium-length blonde hair atop his head and less than an inch of hair on the side. He also had a short beard and wore a brown leather winter coat.

"I'm doing what I can," Charlemagne responded.

"My great grandfather did not liberalize our people only to have that oaf return to terrorize us again," the man responded.

"Who was your great grandfather?" Charlemagne questioned.

"Ole Monrad," the man replied.

"Vaer stille, Fridtjof, vil du have at den kommisar skal rapportere dig til kongen?" Lars replied to the man in a fearful voice before turning to Charlemagne. "Let us go."

Charlemagne looked at Lars, partially understanding what he had said in Danish. He looked at him with a slightly betrayed face but followed him off the docks.

"Ja," Fridtjof said, "let us go," he mimicked.

Act 6, Scene 4

Charlemagne lit the coal in the fire hole and then stood back as the coal burned. He waited with the miners for several minutes until the water started to boil and pistons started to move. Charlemagne then closed the compartment door and looked to the miners. The miners stood behind him with lanterns at their hands.

"Make sure the engine does not get too hot or it might explode," Charlemagne warned the miners. "I'll let Lars know in case you don't understand me…"

Charlemagne then picked up a cloth on the ground to wipe his grease-laden hands. He then proceeded to walk out of the mine tunnels on his own, coming to the surface as the winter twilight was about to end and go into another long, dark night.

The castle grounds were quiet. Charlemagne looked to the chapel and could see that there were lights inside. He walked over and up the steps, opening the door and entering inside. The inside of the church was cold, but he had not been in here before, so he took slow steps as he looked around at the beautiful decorations about.

The castle chapel had a beautiful stained-glass window ahead and on the lateral sides next to the pews. At the front of the church was Kristoffer, kneeling in prayer. There was a scent of myrrh and an ambience of silence. Charlemagne made the sign of the cross as he entered into the chapel and knelt down. He then looked over to Kristoffer who was deep in a prayer.

The doors then opened behind the two of them. Charlemagne turned around to see Lars. Lars walked over to Charlemagne and held a worried face.

"Mr. Cabernet, if you will please," Lars said, looking over to Kristoffer. "I have some bad news," he whispered. "May we speak outside?"

Charlemagne nodded.

"What bad news?" Kristoffer questioned in his loud voice, standing up and turning around. "What is wrong?"

"My king, I'm afraid some of the villagers have been quite vocal about the lack of food due to the fish in the sea being laced with poisons. They have all rallied together and decided to go home to their families in New Hvitrnord."

"Fools!" Kristoffer shouted. "Do they not see as I see? Are their minds not oriented correctly?! There is only one Hvitrnord and this is their home. For the goodness of our Lord and the people of the world, they must make their sacrifices!"

Kristoffer walked towards them.

"My wife did not die for this town to die with it," Kristoffer claimed. "I will not disappoint her."

Kristoffer then walked past them. The two followed him out of the castle. In the courtyard, Kristoffer turned to them.

"Prepare my sled, and we will travel to the village so that I may speak with them."

"There are only a few dogs left, my king," Lars stated. "The villagers took the rest…"

"Then take what we have and go!" Kristoffer shouted.

Charlemagne looked to Kristoffer with worry and then to Lars who left.

• •

Once the sled was ready, Lars was left behind while Charlemagne and Kristoffer travelled out of the castle and made the hour-long journey to New Hvitrnord. There, they travelled to the center of the town where Kristoffer took looked to Charlemagne.

"Fetch some wood, Karlmann," Kristoffer requested. "We will create a bonfire and rally the people."

Charlemagne nodded. Kristoffer proceeded to shout in Danish in a mighty voice, "*Kom og hor din konge!*"

The villagers slowly poured out of their homes as Charlemagne found some wood and set it down in the town center. Kristoffer ordered some men to help him and within a couple of minutes, they had a medium-sized bonfire. Charlemagne then stood separate from the villagers as Kristoffer paced around in silence.

"*Hvad er betydningen af jul?*" Kristoffer questioned. "*Det er at give og dele i Guds kærlighed. Hvorfor hader du dette? Alt hvad jeg vil er at dele i Guds kærlighed til verden, som vi engang gjorde. Hvorfor har du forladt denne vision? Vores vision? Hvitrnord var engang en nordstjerne, hvor drømmene til de små blev gjort. Hvitrnord i nord er dit hjem. Ikke dette. Vil du ikke bringe smil til de små drenge og piger fra Grønland? Du skylder mig at betale for synderne fra dine forfædre, der opgav min Klara. Hvem forlod mig og overlod os til vores skæbne!*"

"*Vi vil være i fred!*" Fridtjof replied from the back. "*Vores hjem er ikke meget, men det er vores hjem. Her er vi frie, og folket hersker. Vi er et demokrati. Ikke et diktatur!*"

"*Nej, du tager fejl. Du er ingenting!*" Kristoffer shouted. "*Jeg er din konge og hersker. Du vil lære at adlyde mig! I elendige hunde ved intet - se på dette sted og åbn dine øjne! Dit selvstyre har givet dig en ghetto og afhængighed af et fremmed land! Du er ikke fri!*"

Kristoffer took a thin wooden plank from the bonfire and picked it up.

"*Her er din frihed!*" Kristoffer stated, tipping the wooden plank into the home behind him and letting it catch on fire.

Charlemagne's eyes widened. The villagers began to murmur to each other while another shouted and screamed with agony. Kristoffer began to walk to another house.

"*Du tyrann!*" Fridjtof shouted. "*Døden for kongen!*"

Fridtjof then charged towards Kristoffer as Kristoffer walked around the bonfire to the next house. Kristoffer simply gave him his back hand with a mighty force. Fridtjof flew backwards and landed on the hard snow. Kristoffer then made his way to another home and then the one behind the villagers and one to their side. He went from home to home and then tossed the log into the bonfire and looked to the villagers as they spread out and panicked. Charlemagne looked at Kristoffer. There was a red glow on his face from the fire. His eyes were dark, but he had a satisfactory smile on his face.

"*Når du er færdig med at græde, venter dit sande hjem på dig i nord og på bakken,*" Kristoffer said to them as they continued to panic. "*Alle velkomne. Inkluderet forræderen midt i dig. Der er meget arbejde, der skal gøres i dit sande hjem, så græd hurtigt.*"

Kristoffer then walked away from the bonfire and passed Charlemagne.

"Karlmann, let us leave. There is nothing to see here."

Charlemagne looked at all the villagers in distress and followed Kristoffer back to the sled. He boarded and then the two went away from the village and northwards to Old Hvitrnord.

Act 7, Scene 1

Two days later, on Christmas Eve, Charlemagne sat at a desk in his room and wrote in a notebook. He was making comments on his conclusions of the fish, which was contaminated not only pesticides, but also lead and a variety of other contaminants brought on through extensive oil fracking and natural gas extraction.

Once Charlemagne was finished, he put his notebook in his backpack and moved his backpack over to his luggage. The castle vibrated. Charlemagne paused where he stood and then grabbed his coat. He looked around, expecting another vibration, but there was none. He then left his room and proceeded to wander around the castle.

Charlemagne passed the great hall where there were various villagers piled inside with blankets around themselves and miserable faces. Charlemagne paused to look inside and saw all the different people, women and children, boys and girls, babies and infants. They all seemed to have miserable expressions on themselves. All Charlemagne could do was sigh. He then went towards the factory, but there was no activity inside. The toy production, short as it was, had ended for the day and the villagers were resting.

From the factory, Charlemagne went down a corridor to go outside to the courtyard. There, he saw Lars coming from the castle gates and over to him.

"Mr. Cabernet, something terrible has happened," Lars said to him. "Come."

"What now?" Charlemagne questioned, following Lars out of the castle.

"It is hopeless now, Mr. Cabernet," Lars said. "First off, there was a terrible explosion in the mines earlier. The machine you fixed exploded, but thankfully nobody was hurt as the miners got out in time, but there was a cave-in in the tunnel we were digging and the machine is now beyond repair."

"Good grief," Charlemagne remarked.

"There is more," Lars stated. "The bridge between the town and the fjord collapsed suddenly, and we are unsure what was the cause."

"Interesting," Charlemagne replied. "Let me take a look at the wreckage."

Charlemagne arrived at the docks and he was then led onto the ice. The two walked over to the ruins of the bridge where Charlemagne began to look around.

"Kristoffer will not be pleased with us," Lars said. "I went to you first because I know I could trust you, but he will find out eventually…"

"Calm down," Charlemagne told Lars. "All will be calm."

"How long until he begins to kill us one by one for our incompetence?" Lars questioned. "How long? What if he thinks that these were the actions of rebels?"

Charlemagne sighed and refused to answer. He continued to search the ruins before looking over to the coast. The icy layer the town was built on sat atop some exposed rock that Charlemagne had not seen earlier. Charlemagne walked over to the plateau and examined the rock.

"My God," Charlemagne remarked, looking over to Lars. "Hvitrnord is not built upon the earth. It's built on a glacier…"

Charlemagne began to walk deeper into the fjord, following the coastline to see that the pattern was rampant throughout. He then returned to Lars.

"Well?" Lars questioned.

"Hvitrnord was built on a glacier…" Charlemagne said to him. "What time was the explosion at the mine?"

"About less than an hour ago..." Lars said. "I could not tell you beforehand because this happened next. Oh, everything is falling apart..."

Charlemagne and Lars looked over to the coastline as they heard a terrible roar occur in the background. The noise echoed around them. Charlemagne looked at the edge between the ice and the rock to see a slight movement.

"Good Lord," Charlemagne swore. "Listen carefully. I want you to gather all the villagers and get them out of the town. Hvitrnord is not safe. I will speak to the king and tell him of what I have discovered. I will then contact my people to get us out of here, okay? Can you rally the people?"

"Yes, Mr. Cabernet. Of course," Lars said to him.

"Good, now go," Charlemagne replied, looking back over to the coastline. "Now, I need to speak to the king, but first... I need to find the kids."

Charlemagne took a step back and then went down the coast and towards the docks. He then went into the village again and to the castle. Once inside the castle, he went to the rooms of the children. He opened the door and barged in on Diana and Tristan who were sitting next to each other on a bed.

"Children, I'm afraid I have some bad news..." Charlemagne stated.

Charlemagne then quickly explained about what had happened.

"Pack your things and then go to my room to retrieve my items. Bring them to a sled and have the dogs pull it out to a clearing on the other side of the fjord. Once you have done that, wait there for the helicopter. I'm going to contact the Ingstad and have them send that helicopter out. We're leaving, understood?"

"Yes, sir," Tristan replied.

"Good man," Charlemagne responded. "Now, get to it."

"Wait, what are you going to do?" Diana questioned.

"I have to go speak with the king," Charlemagne replied. "Kristoffer will have to listen to reason. There is no means for him to deliver those toys of his to all of Greenland – his vision has been a failure and it is time to exodus."

Charlemagne then left the room and went out to the courtyard. He crossed the grounds, looking into the chapel, but did not see Kristoffer there. He went into the tower and proceeded to go up to the king's bedroom, but there was no answer at the door and the room was empty. Charlemagne then walked down to the courtyard again and crossed over to go up the stairs and down a corridor towards the factory. He then entered and went down to Kristoffer's private workshop. There, Charlemagne knocked on the door.

"*Hvar er det?*" Kristoffer questioned.

"It's me, Charlemagne," Charlemagne stated. "We need to talk."

Charlemagne entered the workshop and then paused as he looked around him. The workshop was small, about the same size as the one aboard the Ludendorff in fact. However, this workshop had stained-glass windows on either side and extensive workbenches with smaller machines atop of them. The room was cold and not heated.

Almost the entire room was filled with small ice statues. The statues were depictions of Klara, Kristoffer's wife, in various poses and detailed just as she appeared to Charlemagne. Charlemagne took a deep sigh and then looked over to Kristoffer who had his back to him, sat on a stool, hunched over and working.

"Kristoffer, there is an emergency," Charlemagne stated to him.

"What emergency?" Kristoffer questioned.

"For a start, activities in the mines were forced to come to a halt because the excavator machine exploded. Nobody was injured, however, the extensive mining and now this explosion has caused the glacier this town was built upon to start to slide towards the ocean."

"What does that even mean?"

"A glacier is a block of ice left behind from the ice age. These blocks of ice rest upon the earth and usually stick to it, but due to the activities of the mine, there is nothing anchoring the block of ice to the earth. These blocks have existed for thousands of years across the northern hemisphere, our part of the world, and unfortunately, when your ancestors came to this area and built their town here, they built it upon a glacier."

The castle began to vibrate. Kristoffer ignored it.

"Bah, it is common," Kristoffer remarked in a depressed voice. "I have lived for sixty years before I was frozen. It is a common occurrence."

Charlemagne rolled his eyes.

"Listen, Kristoffer, you need to listen. Your people are in danger – this entire town is going to collapse in the next hour or so because the vibrations are only going to get worse."

"What time is it?"

"About an hour to two o'clock," Charlemagne responded, looking at his watch. "Why?"

"My God!" Kristoffer shouted, standing up. "I need to leave!"

"Yes," Charlemagne agreed.

"I have to deliver the presents!" Kristoffer added.

"No," Charlemagne rejected as Kristoffer passed him.

Charlemagne followed him out of the workshop.

"Stop!" Charlemagne shouted at him. "Listen to me!"

Kristoffer stopped and then turned around with an annoyed face. He walked over to Charlemagne.

"Do you dare speak in such a way to me?" Kristoffer questioned. "Make no mistake, Karlmann, I have great respect for you, but you do *not* speak to me in such a manner. I am the royal king of these lands."

"You are an idiot!" Charlemagne replied. "Your people are in danger of being homeless and all you can think about is your mission? To deliver presents to children? My God, you really are a tyrant and a miserable oaf. You are not a king. A king is a leader – someone who protects his people from danger and cares for them."

"I am caring for my people – all the people of Greenland."

"Your care for strangers beyond your proximity is taking a toll on the people closest to you – your neighbors – those close to you!" Charlemagne argued. "You have lived under the ice for ninety years, but you still do not understand that it is not the thirties anymore. Greenland is different to how it once was – it is no longer as it was. A new and abundance of people have made this island that was once of the Danes, your ancestors, their home; an entire nation of a new people with a new culture and identity who would be estranged to you, an outsider. They would not welcome you as you expect, nor is to your cross to care for these people even if your pride says so. Home is where your people are, your neighbors, who share your descendants with, and the only common people you have left are these people – the descendants of the ancestors that your wife loved! You must love your neighbors, not strangers afar!"

"Oh, you are crazed, Karlmann," Kristoffer remarked, turning his back on him and walking away. "The people are not as weak as I said they were. They would never let such a fate fall upon them. The spirit of the Greenlander will live on and on as a proud united nation."

"Please, Kristoffer," Charlemagne replied, "I implore you. Abandon this fable of yours and save your people. Let them leave and I will offer them and yourself refuge in my hometown. I can even offer you work and there you can do good and enact this vision of yours on a greater scale."

"I am not interested."

Charlemagne went after him. Kristoffer stopped at the exit and turned to Charlemagne.

"Is everything set for my adventure outwards?"

"The presents are loaded on the sleigh," Charlemagne replied, "but even then, you have no reindeer. You are not a Santa Claus. Greenland is a big island and it will take you days to venture over the entire island and go from village to village."

"I do not intend to go by dog or by reindeer," Kristoffer replied. "I intend to go by that flying contraption you brought me on here. There is ample space inside that flying machine to put my toys and go from village to village."

"You can't be serious," Charlemagne laughed, "and do you expect me to comply?"

"You will," Kristoffer responded, producing a knife from his belt and waving it at him. "You have no choice. Either the helicopter comes for me, or it comes for the people to leave. You now have no choice, my friend. The helicopter must come and when it does, it will be mine."

Charlemagne frowned at him. He brought a hand to the satellite radio clipped to his belt.

"You have no choice," Kristoffer repeated. "If you want the people to live, you must make the call knowing that I will only take it, but you will do it because you won't damn the people."

"No," Charlemagne replied, looking over to him as he retrieved the radio. "I won't. I'm not a monster. I came for what I needed – the precious metals that you promised me. I knew you had none left, but I stayed out of hope and then out of charity for the people and yourself. I stayed because I was worried and I cared. I have done nothing but that, and that is what my precious years of leadership experience has taught me."

Kristoffer frowned at him. Charlemagne extended the antennae of the radio and turned it on. He then held down the switch and brought the radio close to his mouth.

"Ingstad, this is Charlie-One, requesting immediate exfil at these coordinates, Latitude: Eight-Two-Seven-Five-Zero-Zero; Longitude: Negative Four-Six-Nine-One-Seven-Six. Do you copy?"

Charlemagne waited a second for a response.

"Charlie-One, this is Captain Raleigh of the Research Vessel Ingstad, copying your coordinates. ETA sixty minutes, over and out."

Kristoffer then left. Charlemagne followed him to the courtyard, but not into the tower. Instead, he went over to the great hall where Lars, the kids, and the villagers were getting ready to leave. Charlemagne then went over the kids and met them at the sled.

"Kristoffer is going to his room to prepare to leave for his mission," Charlemagne informed them. "I've contacted the helicopter and it'll be here in about an hour or so. I'll keep an eye on the window for when Kristoffer leaves. I'll then give the signal, and when I go, tell Lars to get the villagers out through the rear. Understood?"

"Yes, sir," Tristan replied, "but we only have this one sled and we're using it to pull all of our crap…"

"Damn, that's right. The other twenty dogs are going to be pulling Kristoffer's sleigh…" Charlemagne replied. "Nonetheless, lead the people out by foot. It's a short distance, less than two kilometers. They'll be able to make it within forty minutes. Make space for the elderly if you can – they don't have any belongings anyways, the poor folks."

"What are we going to do with them?" Tristan questioned. "Are they coming with us?"

"Of course," Charlemagne replied, looking to the kids. "Children, look to the people in this room and look at them closely. They are no different from us because they're just like you or me, but their situation is difficult and they need us. We must love them as we love ourselves because they are close to us and in need of our assistance."

Diana looked to Charlemagne. She nodded.

"I'm going to confront Kristoffer one last time when the helicopter arrives, and I hope he sees reason. All of them are going to come with us to the Ingstad, and from there to Allabrese."

"What if Kristoffer doesn't see reason?" Tristan asked.

Charlemagne shrugged.

"I'll have Allodia contact the Danish government, Canadian government, the Global Defense Project? Anybody – I won't let anything happen to any of you, understood?"

"Yes," Diana replied.

Tristan nodded.

"Good," Charlemagne responded, walking away from them.

Charlemagne went to Lars who was with Fridtjof. He quickly explained to them the plan and they agreed to it. Afterwards, Charlemagne left to sit watch for when Kristoffer exited. The people were ready to leave and Charlemagne had prepared to himself what he intended to say to Kristoffer. Charlemagne's ears then twitched.

The rotors of the helicopter could be heard. Charlemagne backed away and went into the dining hall. He signaled to the Fridtjof and Lars that the helicopter was here. He then left to go outside and meet Kristoffer at the sleigh.

Kristoffer appeared from his tower dressed in his red coat and red hat. He also wore his black boots and mittens. He looked at Charlemagne.

"Hmph," Kristoffer remarked, going over to the sleigh to take the reins.

The sleigh then slid off with him aboard. Charlemagne was silent, looking back to the castle as the villagers began to exit from inside. Once they were halfway, Charlemagne looked to the side and over to the helicopter which landed on the ice in the fjord. He gave a sigh and reached into his coat.

"Please, reconsider, Kristoffer," Charlemagne said in a calm voice. "A better life awaits in my hometown. There, you can do more than what you'll have done on this Christmas Eve."

Kristoffer was silent. Charlemagne sighed and produced the Walther P38 pistol from within his coat. He then pointed it to the king.

"Bring this sleigh back to the castle at once," Charlemagne commanded as they went downhill towards the ice of the fjord.

"You mad man!" Kristoffer remarked, looking at the pistol. "Do you dare bring arms to the king?"

Charlemagne shot a bullet into the sky, which caused the dogs to howl and panic.

"No!" Kristoffer shouted as the dogs panicked along the ice. He pulled at the reins.

Charlemagne then pointed the gun at him again. Kristoffer immediately responded by grabbing Charlemagne at the throat.

Charlemagne choked and dropped the gun. It let off another shot, which startled the dogs. The sleigh began to turn to the left along the ice. Kristoffer threw Charlemagne off and he slid along the ice, defeated just as Fridtjof was two days prior.

The sleigh continued down along the ice and towards the helicopter.

"Dammit," Charlemagne remarked as he laid on his side.

Charlemagne slowly stood up and then began to rush down the half mile stretch. The sleigh stopped approximately twenty feet from the helicopter. The cargo helicopter had its rear open, but there was no sight of Gerald. Charlemagne could see the Kristoffer had the pistol in his right hand as he unloaded the bags of toys. Charlemagne continued to run towards the sleigh, clutching his side.

Kristoffer then exited from the rear of the helicopter and made his way back to the sleigh for more. By then, Charlemagne had begun to catch up. Kristoffer let go of the bags he had and pointed the gun towards Charlemagne. His shot missed. His second shot also missed.

Charlemagne charged towards the king and he tackled him. Kristoffer immediately responded by pushing him back and then punching Charlemagne across the face, causing him to slide back on the ice. Charlemagne stood himself up from the ice and spat out some blood. He then looked to his side and Kristoffer made his approach to him. He grabbed him and brought him over to the sleigh. He then proceeded to tie him down.

"That'll be enough out of you," Kristoffer remarked. "Sit tight."

Gerald came out of the helicopter and looked over to Kristoffer.

"What's all the commotion out here?" Gerald questioned.

"Back inside, or better yet, grab some bags," Kristoffer stated, pointing the pistol at him. "We have many trips to make across Greenland tonight."

"What?" Gerald questioned. "Oh my God – Charles!"

"Enough!" Kristoffer shouted to him. "Do as I ask! I order you!"

Gerald complied and helped Kristoffer. Once the toys were loaded, Kristoffer grabbed Charlemagne and threw him into the back of the helicopter.

"W-where are we going?" Gerald asked as he sat in the cockpit.

"To the nearest village from here," Kristoffer stated, sitting in the cockpit with him. "Hurry."

The helicopter began to lift off. Charlemagne lay on his side in silence. The helicopter rotors span and within twenty minutes, the helicopter began to lower. Kristoffer stood up from his seat and walked over to the doors as they opened. He grabbed a bag of toys and then left the two in the helicopter.

"Mr. Cabernet," Gerald said, "are you alright?"

"I'm fine," Charlemagne said in a weak voice. "Where have you taken us?"

"To a village like he asked," Gerald said.

"Which one?"

"The nearest settlement on my GPS was Etah…"

"Perfect," Charlemagne responded, sitting up.

"Shall I contact Captain Raleigh? Allodia?"

"Not yet," Charlemagne responded, standing up.

Charlemagne left the helicopter and walked out. He then looked over to where Kristoffer was standing, in the midst of the rancid and ugly village, less pleasant than village Kristoffer had burned down. The headlights of the helicopter lit the scene ahead. It was peak darkness and the pale moon was out. Before

Kristoffer was a small Inuit, or perhaps mixed-race child as it was possible although unclear; standing before him with a thick parka on. She looked forward to Kristoffer with a look of stupefaction, mouth slightly open. However, this was not the cause for concern. Behind the child were two Inuit men in thick coats with rifles pointed towards them and belligerence in their eyes. Charlemagne stopped right before Kristoffer as they stared these people down.

The men shouted out towards Kristoffer in Inuit.

"*Jeg har medbragt legetøj til børnene!*" Kristoffer remarked. "*Venligst tag og spred glæden!*"

The Inuit men shouted back in their own language, which neither Charlemagne nor Kristoffer understood. They continued to point their rifles at them.

"Do you see now?" Charlemagne asked, walking over to him with a limp and placing his hand on Kristoffer's arm.

Kristoffer was silent.

"The world changes," Charlemagne confessed. "Sometimes, there are changes that we simply cannot control and have to let be. If you were to go to the next village, you wouldn't see the smiling boys and girls that you envision who would welcome you with open arms. You would instead see this sort of belligerence – folks who are suspicious of people like us. Such is the trend up here nowadays if not in the wider world; a society of mistrust and lack of social cohesion. Like I said, Greenland is no longer an island of the Nords as it once was, nor is the rest of the world."

"I've been a fool," Kristoffer confessed to himself, looking straight forward to their foes. "I may have been entrapped in ice, but even after you had rescued me, I continued to be in a state of a deep freeze," he said, before looking to Charlemagne "My

God! And my people… they are in trouble…!" he added with alert. "We must go at once!"

"Yes," Charlemagne responded, nodding "and they'll be gone if you don't return this instant."

Kristoffer nodded and then left with Charlemagne as they slowly backed away. The two then turned around and went towards the helicopter where they entered through the rear.

"There's nothing wrong with having a vision, or even owning a business, Kristoffer," Charlemagne said to him, "but as long as you continue to regard your people as your primary priority. Come to Allabrese with me, and you will learn and be able to make your vision – Klara's vision come true."

Act 7, Scene 2

The cargo helicopter began to make its return to Hvitrnord where Charlemagne could see the people grouped on the other side of the fjord like he had asked. On the other side, the glacier of the town had slipped onto the docks and one of the towers of the castle had collapsed. The helicopter began to make its descent and came to a halt. Charlemagne then went around to the back where Kristoffer was already taking the sacs of toys in each hand.

The doors then opened and Kristoffer walked out with the sacs, dropping them on the snow. The people took a step back as they saw him appear.

"My people," Kristoffer shouted, "hurry onto this contraption! It will take you to safety – come along!"

"Is this a joke?" Fridtjof questioned.

"No," Charlemagne responded, clutching his side as he came down the ramp, "now hurry! We're running low on fuel and need to get to the ship as fast as possible!"

Charlemagne went over to the kids and helped them unload the sled with their belongings. Diana put her bags behind the cockpit seats. She then returned to help, but there was nothing left. Tristan came too and saw a nutcracker on the snow, pouring out from the sac of toys. He picked it up as Charlemagne returned to guide the kids inside the helicopter before he went to help Kristoffer load all the other townsfolk into the craft. Only about half of the population could have sat with the seniors taking priority over the youth. The others were forced to stand. In total, there were less than a hundred in the helicopter. Charlemagne budged his way through to the cockpit once everybody was aboard. He then signaled Gerald to take-off.

Gerald raised the helicopter off from the ice and began to hover upwards.

From within the helicopter, the crack of the ice could be heard from outside. Charlemagne looked out of the cockpit window as the ice began to crash into the ocean and slip away. Kristoffer and the kids looked out of the cargo hold portholes. Kristoffer held a sadder face than anyone else on the helicopter. Tristan looked at him before looking over to Diana. He took out the nutcracker from within his coat and handed it to Diana.

"Here," Tristan said, handing the nutcracker to Diana, "here's our souvenir for this adventure. A little memento from Santa's Workshop. Merry Christmas."

Diana took the toy into her hand. She looked at its fine details. The nutcracker was dressed in a red suit with a black cap and moustache. Diana smiled and then gave Tristan a kiss on his cold cheek. She then stood up and went to her bag, retrieving a small blue box. She then went over to Tristan to hand it to him.

"Here," Diana said, handing it to him.

Tristan took the box and pulled the silver ribbon. He then opened the top and uncovered the white tissue paper. Inside the box was a small piece of alien alloy that was almost shaped like a heart.

"Where did you get this?" Tristan questioned.

"From the asteroid wreckage last summer," Diana answered. "I saved it – it was our meteorite, wasn't it? The one you made your wish on. I thought it would be special to you – to us."

Tristan smiled and stood up, giving Diana a kiss on the cheek and a hug.

"Yes," Tristan said, "it is special. Thank you."

Charlemagne sat back in his cockpit seat and gave a sigh of relief. Tristan and Diana came around to join him once they put their gifts away in their luggage.

"Are you okay?" Tristan asked, looking at the beat up state of Charlemagne.

"Yes," Charlemagne responded. "I am. I'm sorry…"

"Stop," Diana replied. "You don't need to apologize for this adventure. We're used to them not going as intended."

Charlemagne looked to her and nodded.

"Let's get to the boat – this has been one hell of a Christmas Eve and I need to have a lie down…" Charlemagne said, sighing again. "More importantly, let's get out of this desolate place for good."

"Aye," Tristan responded, "but what about the Ludendorff?"

"Oh, we'll worry about that tomorrow or better yet, the day after tomorrow. I'm sure Gerald here won't mind if we fly out for another trip, or better yet, I'm sure Allodia won't mind. Right?"

Charlemagne laughed as he looked over to Gerald who looked back at him with an unsure face. The helicopter continued to roll across the lands and return to the Ingstad to celebrate Christmas the only way it can be celebrated, with care and with one's common folk.

Epilogue

Charlemagne and Kristoffer stood on the portside of the Ingstad, looking out to the Arctic Ocean three days after Christmas.

"I left everything behind," Kristoffer said, reminiscing.

"You took what was important," Charlemagne replied, "and you will be given more riches than what was possible in these lands."

"Yes," Kristoffer agreed, "you are right. I hope they have a better life in your hometown."

"You will," Charlemagne assured him.

"I hope the people can forgive me."

"In time, they should," Charlemagne said. "You've given them opportunity."

"I was wrong about what the meaning of Christmas was," Kristoffer said. "I thought it was about giving and sharing, but that is far from the truth. The simple truth – so simple, was love itself just as our Lord died on the cross."

Charlemagne nodded and looked out to the plains of ice.

"My Klara… she is with the Lord now," Kristoffer said, looking up and to the skies.

Across the night skies were the dancing northern lights in their blue-green palette. Charlemagne looked at the skies and smiled.

"You know, they look like ghosts," Charlemagne remarked to him, "but on a larger scale and stretched out."

"What are you talking of?" Kristoffer questioned.

"Nevermind," Charlemagne said to him, "you wouldn't understand."

Charlemagne turned behind him and looked as the kids came around to join him. Tristan wore a handcrafted traditional Nordic sweater that was gifted to him by old Mrs. Jensen. It was light grey with various patterns, crosses, and dots in white. The rim at where there were buttons at the top going up to the neck hole was red with a distinct pattern in pink. Meanwhile, Diana wore a touphe similar to Kristoffer's, but in a darker red.

"Well, Diana, do you still believe in climate change?" Tristan asked her.

Diana shrugged.

"Climate change?" Charlemagne questioned.

Diana and Tristan looked at each other before looking at Charlemagne.

"Charles, you're a scientist," Diana said. "What can you tell us about climate change?"

Charlemagne took a deep breath as he looked out of the ship.

"Well, it's a complicated topic, Diana. Nobody really knows what causes the climate to change any more than we know why or how the dinosaurs were wiped out. One thing is for sure, and that is that climates do change, but whether humans are behind that change is unlikely and most data around the 'global warming' narrative is not on a large-scale necessarily and typically only from a couple of years."

"And now that we've been in the artic for some time," Tristan added, "you can see that it's not melting. The fact that Hvitrnord went down under was out of more serious concerns of reckless resource extraction. And from a figurative standpoint, due to pollution since the people couldn't eat anything because of all the pollutants in the water."

"Melting?" Kristoffer interrupted. "My beautiful home, melting?"

Kristoffer laughed.

"Children, you should have seen these lands when my ancestors first came a thousand years ago! There was nowhere near this much ice and snow!" Kristoffer jeered, laughing some more. "Ho, ho, ho!"

"Yes, that's right," Charlemagne nodded, "I suppose when his ancestors came to Greenland it was the medieval warming period – temperatures then were much higher in this part of the world than they are now. That's just the way the climate works... unpredictably."

Charlemagne looked to the kids.

"To be honest, in my opinion, climate trends are difficult to predict. My own research has suggested that the sun is the most likely culprit behind these random trends, and with increased solar activity, a global warming is likely, but only as much as the sun would like it to be. The sun itself is unpredictable. If you want to learn more, I can refer to you the research of a colleague of mind from Sweden."

"No, I'm good," Diana sighed. "Tristan can win this one, but in fairness, I won the bet on Santa Claus."

Tristan stuck his tongue out at her.

"Santa Claus?" Kristoffer questioned. "Who is this Santa Claus?"

"Bet?" Charlemagne himself questioned, looking at the kids with a frown. "You came here because of a bet?"

"Well, look at the time," Tristan said, grabbing Diana's wrist, "it's time for bed. See you, Charles! See you, Kris!"

Diana and Tristan quickly left while Allodia came to join them.

"Where are those two going?" Allodia questioned.

"Shamelessly bouncing off, it appears," Charlemagne replied, smiling at his sister.

"Wow, look at that," Allodia remarked to the lights. "I was hoping we'd get to see them before we left."

"Yes, it is quite a sight," Charlemagne agreed, looking up to the skies.

"Allodia, thank you for your hospitality," Kristoffer said to her. "Thank you for taking in all of my folk and taking us to your hometown."

"It's no problem," Allodia replied, smiling to him. "I'm always happy to take in a couple more guests... or ten, or a hundred. Let's not forget to mention all those robots and guns in the cargo hold now..."

"Yes," Charlemagne replied, "I think I better leave."

"Not so fast, Charlie," Allodia responded, "because you've wasted so much fuel, you're going to pay for the refueling we'll be doing in Iceland."

"Very well..." Charlemagne sighed, "I might as well take the kids around there and perhaps invite Judith over."

"Good," Allodia smiled, "and on the topic of Judith, she wants to talk to you, so go speak with her on the phone when you have the chance and before we lose our signal."

"She does? What of?"

"Something to do with an award you are going to be given," Allodia replied. "Sorry, not you, but for our grandfather. She said it was some sort of award given to French people for their services."

"Really?" Charlemagne questioned. "Amazing."

"On that note, I have some good news for you, Kris," Allodia said. "I was doing some research of my own and think I've located your son – or at least, the legacy of your family."

"What?" Kristoffer questioned.

"Yeah, apparently, you weren't quite forgotten by your son. You see, in Denmark, there is a renowned worldwide toy company whose founder came from Greenland. Apparently, his father went missing one day and after the world war, the

Americans occupied his home and he came to work hard labor for them with their oil extraction. He saved the money he earned and went to the United States to study engineering, and when he returned, his skills with oil allowed him to synthesize a special type of plastic. With this patent, he made millions and with those millions, he turned his hobby of toy-making into a worldwide business. The founder of this company was Kristoff Kristoffersen. Unfortunately, he appears to have passed on in the nineties, but the current owner of the company is his grandson, your great grandson, Kristian Kristoffersen."

Kristoffer gave a heartwarming smile and nodded.

"Do you want to meet them?" Allodia asked.

Kristoffer's eyes widened. He looked to Allodia and he shook his head.

"No, I don't think that would be appropriate," Kristoffer said, laughing. "I am happy to hear what I have heard, but my son's life was lived and I would be nothing more than a stranger to his descendants. It's enough to know this – that the Kristoffersen line lives on and with it, the life of my wife."

Charlemagne looked to Kristoffer and smiled.

"On that note, I think I'll honestly be retiring for the night," Charlemagne remarked to them. "Goodnight."

"Goodnight, Charlie."

"Goodnight, Charlemagne," Kristoffer said to him, nodding.

Charlemagne returned inside the Ingstad and went to his cabin. He opened the door and looked over to Tristan hunched over his desk and writing in a black book.

"What are you up to?" Charlemagne questioned, raising an eyebrow.

"Oh, nothing," Tristan deflected, closing the book. "What's up?"

"I just heard the most inspiring thing from Allodia in regard to Kristoffer," Charlemagne replied, walking over and sitting down on his bed.

"Oh, really? Tristan questioned, turning in his chair, and smiling to him. "Tell me everything that happened after Diana and I left."

"Best of all, Christmas means a spirit of love when the love of God and the love of our fellow men should prevail over all hatred and bitterness, a time when our thoughts and deeds and the spirit of our lives manifest the presence of God."

– George F. McDougall